# LOVE AT LAST

## A LAST FRONTIER LODGE NOVEL

## J.H. CROIX

# DEDICATION

*This one goes out to my readers for such amazing support - cheers to many more!*

**Sign up for my newsletter for information on new releases!**

*J.H. Croix Newsletter*

**Follow me!**
*jhcroix@jhcroix.com*
*https://amazon.com/author/jhcroix*
*https://www.bookbub.com/authors/j-h-croix*
*https://www.facebook.com/jhcroix*

# CHAPTER 1

*D*elia jumped at the sound of banging on the front door. Reflexively, she glanced around the kitchen though she knew perfectly well no one else was there. It was close to midnight, and she was alone in the kitchen at Last Frontier Lodge. As far as she knew, every guest who had reservations had checked in hours earlier. The ski lodge was booked solid, so if whoever happened to be banging at the door hoped for a room, they were out of luck. She'd stayed late tonight to prep the pastries for breakfast tomorrow. Uncertain who could be here, but aware that it was below zero outside, she brushed the flour off of her hands and made her way through the darkened hall and into the reception area. When she swung the door open, her pulse lunged.

Garrett Hamilton stood in the small circle of light. His glossy dark hair looked as if he'd run a hand through it a few too many times, and his blue eyes were weary. Yet, he was so damn handsome, he stole her breath away. She must have stood there a beat too long with her mouth hanging open because Garrett arched a brow and nudged his chin forward.

"Were you planning to let me freeze out here, or can I come in?"

Delia gave her head a shake and stepped back from the door. "Sorry. You startled me. Come on in." She gestured for him to pass by. Garrett adjusted the bag slung over his shoulder and walked inside. He paused and waited while she closed and bolted the heavy door. When she turned to face him, she felt suddenly self-conscious. Her hair was in a messy ponytail with long curls hanging loosely around her face. Her apron was streaked with the evidence of a day's cooking in a busy ski lodge.

Garrett allowed his bag to fall to the floor and shrugged out of his winter coat. His chest and shoulders stretched at the fabric of his t-shirt underneath. Beyond his knowing blue eyes, his face might as well have been sculpted by an artist with his angular features and sensual mouth.

Delia swallowed and tried get her pulse under control. She'd met Garrett when he was here over Christmas. His brother, Gage Hamilton, was her boss. She supposed Garrett could technically be considered her boss as well since he and the rest of his siblings shared ownership of Last Frontier Lodge with Gage. Garrett cleared his throat. Delia whipped her head up, realizing her eyes had been coasting over his rock-hard abs. She wondered if he knew the effect he had on women.

"Where to?" he asked, his voice gruff.

Delia bit her lip and considered what to do with Garrett. There wasn't a single room available, and Gage hadn't mentioned anything about making sure she kept a room available for Garrett. Along with managing the kitchen at the lodge, she managed the staff for reception and house-keeping. She met Garrett's blue eyes and somehow found her voice.

"Um...did Gage know you were coming?"

Garrett shook his head sharply. "Nope. Tried to call him when I changed planes in Anchorage, but I only got his voicemail. Is it a problem I'm here?"

"Oh, no. I'm just trying to figure out where to put you. The lodge is booked. I'm sure Gage and Marley wouldn't mind if you stayed in the private apartment with them, but I'm guessing they're asleep by now."

Garrett picked up his bag again and turned to walk toward the kitchen. Delia followed behind, wondering where he planned to go. He strode through the kitchen and into her small office beside it. His bag hit the floor with a thump. He turned so quickly, she collided with him. Flushed, she stepped back.

"Sorry. I, um, can I get you something?" Her mind taunted her. *Can you get him something? It's midnight and you're following him around like an idiot.* Garrett flustered her, and the situation made it worse. She'd been working quietly in the kitchen for the last two hours since the kitchen staff went home for the night. The last thing she'd expected was to be facing a guest at this hour. And Garrett Hamilton, no less. She'd thought him all kinds of sexy when she met him when he visited over the holidays. But she'd politely reminded herself he was in another stratosphere.

From what she knew, Garrett was a high-profile corporate lawyer with the money and looks to accentuate his sleek career. She was just a single mother who grew up in Diamond Creek, Alaska. She was doing better than she had in the last few years, but that was mostly thanks to Gage offering her this job. Not only was she finally able to save some money, but she also loved her job. She'd once dreamed of being a chef in a big city, but she found this job as satisfying as any she could have imagined. She had free rein to dream up whatever gourmet dishes she wanted, along with a bustling restaurant filled with ski tourists and locals every night of the week. All of that in the hometown she loved. A place like Diamond Creek was hard to beat—spectacular views of mountains, glaciers and the ocean, along with a bustling business scene with arts and restaurants abounding to meet the demands of tourists who traveled from all over the world to visit Alaska. Throw in the reality that Diamond Creek held onto its small-town charm due to its far-flung, rural location on the wild coast of Alaska, and she couldn't imagine finding a much more charmed place. Though there had been times when she'd chafed at the small world of Diamond Creek, she loved it.

Garrett cleared his throat again. She looked up to find his sharp blue eyes on her. Fighting the flush that heated her face, she met his eyes. "We have tea and hot cider. I was just finishing up when you got here."

Garrett nodded. "Your hot cider?" he asked, the corner of his mouth kicking up into a way-too-charming smile.

Heat swirled in her belly. She nodded.

"Perfect. You think it'll be okay if I crash on the couch in here?" He gestured to the couch along one wall in her office.

She shrugged. "Probably your best option unless you want to wake Gage and Marley." She turned to stride into the kitchen and quickly poured him a mug of cider. It had been cooling, but was still warm enough.

When she handed it to him, Garrett took a swallow and sighed. "Damn. Gage made me try your cider at Christmas. I'm not really a cider guy, but this…" He held his mug up. "… is amazing. It's got a hell of a kick."

Delia flushed and shrugged. "It's my mother's recipe." She fiddled with her necklace and tucked a loose curl behind her ear. "I'll get out of your way now. Some of the kitchen staff will arrive as early as five, so don't get startled."

Garrett took another gulp of cider and grinned. "Right. I'll make sure I'm up and out of the way."

She nodded and pulled her apron off. She quickly

covered the pastries and slid them in the refrigerator. Garrett wandered out to the empty restaurant. She glanced in to see him standing by the windows. When she called goodbye, he turned and waved. For a second, she thought he was going to say something, but he remained silent. She left, making her way out to her car in the dark, cold night. Stars glittered above, sharp in the crisp air. She drove home, wondering why Garrett affected her the way he did. After her youthful tease with love in college, she'd discovered not much in life was guaranteed, most definitely not the fluff of fantasy. Out of the ashes of that painful lesson came her son Nick. He was the single best part of her life, but she'd learned her lesson quite thoroughly and steered clear of relationships.

She hadn't fantasized about a man in years. Until Garrett showed up at the ski lodge over the holidays. His presence was like a lightning bolt. She couldn't help but wonder about his unannounced visit now. With a sharp shake of her head, she turned down the driveway to her father's house. She'd moved home with Nick after barely finishing college. Being a single mother was a financial challenge beyond anything she could have imagined. While she didn't feel great about staying with her father, it was the smartest option she had. She had free child care, and while Nick might not have his father around, he had hers. Her mother had passed away a few years ago. She knew it helped her father to have her and Nick around, so she figured while she may have stashed her dreams of independence and happily-ever-after, at least she could make sure her son and father benefited from each other's presence.

* * *

THE MOON WAS high in the sky, its silvery light bright on the ski slopes. Garrett looked out into the darkness and took another hearty swallow of Delia's amazing cider. She didn't scrimp on the alcohol content, and he savored the burn. The mountains loomed in the darkness, hulking shapes in the night. The waters of Kachemak Bay rippled under the moonlight. Garrett took a deep breath and turned away from the view. He strode back into the kitchen and refilled his mug. He returned to sit by the windows and let the quiet settle around him.

His mind wandered to Delia and he chuckled. Damn, she had no idea what she did to him. When Gage had introduced him to her over the holidays, he'd had to resist the urge to flirt with her. He knew it would annoy Gage, and for some reason, he'd known it was a dangerous place for him to go. She was just so damn sexy and cute. When she answered the door tonight, he wanted to tuck those loose honey gold curls behind her ears and kiss her full lips. But she was not the kind of girl he could do that with. For starters, Delia Peters worked for his brother. She also happened to be a single mother, and the consensus from everyone Garrett encountered in Diamond Creek was that she was just about the nicest woman in the universe. No matter how tempting Delia was, the truth was they were worlds apart. She was a wholesome, small-town single mother. He'd spent years cultivating his reputation as the go-to corporate lawyer in Seattle. That translated to work, work and more work. Relationships were low on his priority list.

He was the master at brief and casual—precisely why the attraction he felt toward Delia confused him. He preferred things to be on his terms. Translation: under his control. Delia was the first woman he'd met who ruffled his composure. For God's sake, he wanted to tease her about the smudge of flour on her cheek. He couldn't remember if he'd *ever* contemplated kissing a woman impulsively. But he'd stood by the window right here and looked across the room at her and wanted more than the quick brush of her soft curves when she bumped into him in the office. He wanted to know how her plump lips felt under his and wanted to see what happened when she let loose. Because he'd bet anything she was something else.

Garrett swore softly and gulped down the rest of his cider, forcing his thoughts away from Delia. He looked around the shadowed restaurant and felt a prick of pride at the work Gage had put into this place. When Gage told him he was moving back to Diamond Creek, Alaska, Garrett had thought he was half-crazy. Garrett had only fuzzy memories of coming to Last Frontier Lodge to visit their grandparents over the holidays. Now that he'd seen what Gage had done, he was impressed. Last Frontier Lodge was well on its way to being the premier ski destination it had once been in its heyday. As for Diamond Creek—well, it was so beautiful it made his chest tighten. He was so accustomed to the bustle of Seattle and the hustle of work, the awe-inspiring beauty of Alaska made him crave the quiet it offered and the way it took him out of the relentless turning wheels of his mind.

He stretched out on the couch in the office he'd commandeered and stared at the ceiling. He pondered how he'd explain his surprise visit to Gage. A bit of a challenge when he wasn't so sure what had driven him to book a flight to Alaska at the last minute. For the first time in years, he'd walked out of a courtroom and instead of being gleeful at the case he'd won, he felt bitter and tired. He'd looked across the room at the woman who'd lost her lawsuit against the insurance company and couldn't even meet her eyes. Next thing he knew, he'd told his assistant to rearrange his entire schedule for the next month and booked a flight to Alaska.

Hours later, Garrett blinked his eyes open and looked around. The wispy light of a cold winter morning filtered into the office. He stretched and stood. Swiping his bag, he quickly stepped into the tiny bathroom adjacent to the office, which conveniently had a shower. He had no idea why, but it worked for him. In record time, changed and refreshed, he walked into the kitchen, glancing at his watch to see it was just past six-thirty. Though there was no one in sight, fresh coffee scented the air. He walked in the direction of the coffee pot when the door beside it swung open.

Delia collided with him. Garrett looked down into her blue eyes. Her honey gold hair fell in tousled waves around her shoulders. The door was behind her now, so she couldn't step back. For the life of him, Garrett couldn't either. Her breasts rose and fell with her breath, the lush curves grazing his chest. Without a thought, he closed the distance between them and brought his lips to hers. She gasped, and he dove into the warm sweetness ofof her mouth. Lust surged through him as he slid his hands down her sides, his thumbs caressing the full curve of her breasts, and around to cup her bottom. He tugged her against him, unable to resist the urge to arch into the cradle of her hips.

She moaned into his mouth, and it was as if she struck a match inside of him. Lust coiled and tightened, the heat of his want for her so strong, all he knew was he wanted more. *Now.* He couldn't have imagined that she'd become a living flame in his arms, her tongue tangling wildly with his, her hands stroking roughly up his chest and dragging down his back. Distantly, he heard voices and tore his lips from hers. He opened his eyes to find hers locked onto him. She took another breath and he had to fight to get his body leashed. He had a raging hard-on and wanted nothing more than to drag her to the office couch and tear her clothes off. So much for control. He took shaky breath and stepped away.

# CHAPTER 2

*D*elia leaned into the backseat of the car, reaching with one arm to find the present Nick had picked out for his friend's birthday. Her fingers slipped on the wrapping paper. She reflexively curled her hand around the gift only to cringe at the sound of paper tearing. With a sigh, she yanked the present forward. Two finger-shaped holes marred the surface. Blue fur taunted her through the holes. Nick had spent close to an hour finding the perfect stuffed whale at a toy store in Anchorage last week. One of the joys of being a single mother was constantly hurrying, constantly feeling as if she wasn't quite measuring up to what her little boy needed. Today's joy was perfectly encapsulated in the fact she'd been in too much of a rush to turn around and look for the damn present. Tears pricked at her eyes.

*Seriously, Delia? It's not a big deal.*

Another sigh and Delia forced her brain to shut up. Some days, it was hard not to get down over little things. She'd learned to let go of so much. Her dream of being a chef at a fancy restaurant somewhere big had been whittled down to its nub. She'd come full circle and now worked in the same kitchen her mother had managed when she was a little girl. She thanked the stars every day that she loved it. Her dream was simply gone, vanished in the harsh light of reality. The familiarity of the kitchen at Last Frontier Lodge offered a comfort she hadn't known she needed. She hadn't imagined being a mother like this—when she could barely pay the bills and constantly hoped she was good enough. When Gage Hamilton had offered Delia her mother's old job at the ski lodge, she'd experienced a mix of euphoria and resignation. Euphoria because she could finally consider finding her own place with a steady income. Resignation because she was treading a familiar path—staying in her hometown and essentially following her mother's footsteps with the glaring exception that Delia hadn't married a steady man such as her father. No, she'd fallen in lust in college and confused it with love. Once she'd settled into her job at the ski lodge, she realized she loved the comfort. She still felt like she was ten steps behind when it came to keeping up with everything she needed to do for Nick, but she did the best she could.

She smoothed out the torn wrapping paper and dug through the glove compartment, grinning when she found a roll of tape. She carefully taped the paper back together and climbed out of the car. Just in time because the school bus pulled up right behind her. Nick came barreling off the bus on the heels of his best friend, Roddy Hale. She'd arranged for him to ride the bus here since she didn't have time to get to school before the bell.

"Mom!"

Nick raced straight for her, flinging his arms around her waist. She ruffled his almost-black hair and dropped a kiss on his head. "Hey sweetie." She pulled away and knelt down. "Do you want to carry Roddy's present inside? Or have me give it to his mom?"

Nick's blue eyes met hers, wide and bright. "I'll carry it," he announced. As soon as she pulled it out from behind her back, he grabbed it and immediately punctured the wrapping paper in another spot. He didn't even notice. Delia chuckled as he whirled away and ran across the lawn to Roddy's house. She followed at a slower pace. Kathryn, Roddy's mother, met her at the door.

"Hey Delia, you staying for the party?"

Delia shook her head. "I have to get to work soon, but I wanted to see if you needed any help with set up."

Kathryn leaned in the doorway. "Thanks for the offer, but I'm keeping it simple this time. I've discovered a roomful of six-year old boys can destroy the best-laid plans. I've got paper plates, plastic cups and beanbags all over the living room. Until it's time to eat, they'll be running loose in the backyard," she offered with a grin and a shrug.

Delia chuckled, a sense of relief washing through her. Kathryn was one of the mothers who made her feel less like a complete mess. "Sounds like a plan. I can pick Nick up around ten tomorrow. Will that be okay?"

Kathryn nodded. "He can stay as long as he needs to. He's such a good kid. Just text me when you're ready to pick him up."

Moments later, Delia climbed back out of her car and headed into Misty Mountain Café. She'd given herself a cushion of time to get to work in case Kathryn needed some help, so now she had time for coffee. Misty Mountain was her favorite local coffee shop, a preference shared by many locals and tourists. She walked into a crowd of people waiting in line. She took her place at the end and glanced around. Misty Mountain was housed in an old Quonset hut. There were many scattered throughout Alaska from its days as a strategic area during World War II. The old huts, utilitarian tubes of corrugated steel, had been refurbished into many uses across Alaska. Misty Mountain was certainly not the only restaurant housed in a Quonset hut. The owners had taken advantage of the cavernous space and decorated it with bright fabrics and artwork.

Delia was idly reading the specials listed on a chalkboard behind the counter when someone tapped her on the shoulder. Turning, she found Marley Adams, an old friend and Gage's new wife, grinning.

"Hey Marley! I just stopped by on my way up to the lodge. Coffee run for Gage and my dad?"

Marley's green eyes crinkled at the corners when her smile expanded. "Yup. They're heading up to install a new heater in one of the ski huts, so I figured I'd pick up some stuff from the bakery and plenty of coffee for them. Is Nick coming with you today?"

Delia shook her head. "Nope. He's at a birthday party through tonight. He'll be worn out tomorrow, that's for sure."

Marley nudged Delia's shoulder. Delia glanced around to see the line moving forward. She took a quick step before turning back.

"Did you know Garrett was coming up for a visit?" Delia blurted out. She couldn't put the brakes on her curiosity about Garrett. Well, it went far beyond curiosity. More like an intense, driving interest. She couldn't stop thinking about his kiss yesterday morning. He'd left her flustered with liquid heat swirling in her belly. She'd been simultaneously relieved and disappointed she hadn't seen him again for the remainder of the day.

Marley shook her head, her auburn hair swishing side to side in its loose ponytail. "Go figure. Garrett was the least likely of Gage's siblings to randomly show up. I told him he was lucky you were working so late that night. If you hadn't been there, he'd have frozen on the porch."

Their conversation paused when they made it to the front of the line. After they both ordered coffees, they grabbed a table by the windows. Delia scanned the familiar view. Growing up in Diamond Creek, sometimes she took for granted its breathtaking location. It sat on the western side of the Kenai Peninsula in Alaska. The Kenai Peninsula was situated in southcentral Alaska, stretching into the pristine waters of the Pacific Ocean. Cook Inlet threaded its way from the ocean into Alaska. Several volcanoes were nearby with mountains encircling the town and rising tall across Kachemak Bay. Diamond Creek lay on the shores of Kachemak Bay, a world-famous fishing location and draw for wilderness lovers and those seeking out glimpses of Alaska's phenomenal vistas. In addition to fishing, hunting, and eco-tourism, Diamond Creek was once again graced with a ski lodge. Delia couldn't help her smile as she considered how happy her father was to be part of the resurrection of Last Frontier Lodge.

"What?" Marley asked.

Delia turned away from the window. "Huh?"

"What's that smile for?"

Delia's smile returned. "Oh, just thinking how happy my dad's been to have the lodge up and running again."

Marley grinned and took a sip of coffee. "I know. Gage couldn't have done it without him, that's for sure. Not to mention, Gage would've been lost in that restaurant without you."

Delia fiddled with a napkin. "Well, it's working out pretty good for me. It's the first time since I've had Nick that I can actually save a little money." She paused and considered her words. Marley was an old friend. Their parents had been close when they were growing up, but Marley had always intimidated Delia a little. She was so damn smart. Until last year when Marley came back and Delia learned she'd been through her own special hell after she got robbed and assaulted, Delia had assumed Marley was living the dream life. While Delia had been silly enough to fall in lust and get pregnant in college. She'd never have known how quickly her dreams of being a chef in a fancy restaurant could be shoved sideways. Just as she'd never have known Nick's entrance into her world could so easily have made everything else seem petty.

She glanced across the table at Marley and shrugged. "I can't tell you how much it meant to have Gage offer me the job. Once upon a time, I wanted to live in the big city like you did, but now I just want to be in the place I love and make sure I can take care of Nick."

Marley's warm green gaze met hers. "The big city isn't all it's cracked up to be. I wish I'd figured that out a little sooner." She paused and glanced out the window. "Looks like Garrett found his way down here." Marley glanced back to Delia. "Did Garrett say anything about why he was here when he showed up the other night?"

"No. When I asked if Gage knew he was coming, he said no. I wondered if you knew."

Marley shook her head. "Nope. When Gage asked him yesterday, Garrett made it seem like he just got this idea he needed a break. But Gage said that's so out of the ordinary for Garrett, he doesn't even know what to think. He's worried, but he doesn't want to pressure Garrett."

Delia's curiosity started to run wild, but she kept her expression bland. "Oh. Huh. I guess maybe you'll figure it out at some point. How long is he staying?"

"That's the weird part. He said he plans to stay at least a month and maybe longer. Garrett hasn't taken a vacation since forever, according to Gage." Marley shrugged and stopped talking, nodding toward the door.

Delia turned and watched Garrett walking into the café. His shoulders flexed with the swing of his arms. His jacket was open, revealing a t-shirt pulled tight across his muscled chest. His dark hair was ruffled from the wind outside. Even across the room, his bright blue eyes were visible.

They landed on her. Instantly, her body tightened, heat racing through her. He walked across the café, his stride long and loose.

"Gage mentioned you might be here," Garrett said by way of greeting with a nod to Marley.

Marley held the takeout tray of coffees aloft. "I'm on a delivery mission. I need to get going actually. I'm glad you're here though. You can keep Delia company." Marley stood and swung her purse over her shoulder. "I'll see both of you later, I'm sure." Her ponytail swished in time with her walk as she left.

In most circumstances, Delia would have found it easy to make polite conversation with a friend's relative. With Garrett, it wasn't so easy. His kiss the other morning had started a simmering heat that quickly turned into a flash fire. She was out of practice with kisses, much less with managing this wild attraction to Garrett.

She forced a smile when she glanced up at him. "Planning to get a coffee?"

Garrett's smile was slow and sensual. "Hello to you too. Coffee's the reason I'm here. Any suggestions?"

Delia felt silly that she hadn't even bothered to say hello. The flush already heating her face got hotter. "Right. Hello, um… Pretty much everything's good here. You can go with basic coffee or something fancier. Their pastries are really good too."

Garrett hooked his thumb in the belt loop of his jeans, the weight tugging his jeans down just enough to reveal a flash of rock hard abs. Delia's eyes flicked down and immediately back up. Garrett's blue eyes watched her steadily. A glimmer of something flickered in his eyes. "I'll be right back," he said abruptly before swinging away and walking to the counter.

Delia's breath came out in a whoosh. Her heart pounded and flutters danced in her belly. Now would be the time to get a grip. She was acting like an idiot—the same idiot who'd let her body's impulses wreak havoc with her heart in college. *Okay, Delia. He's just a man. Nothing more. Maybe he's sexy, but that's all it is.*

She took several gulps of coffee and fruitlessly attempted to get her pulse to slow down. Several moments later, Garrett slid into the chair across from her. She glanced up into his sharp blue eyes. What little control she'd re-established over her pulse was immediately lost. Her pulse galloped and her breath went short.

He took a swallow of coffee. He set the cup down and sighed. "Damn. That's some good coffee." He looked out the window for a long moment. When his eyes met hers again, they held a hint of weariness. "It's so beautiful here. Gage was the only one of us to really remember much about Alaska. I remember coming to visit at the holidays, but the last time we came was when I was only eight. It's funny how you can't really appreciate some things until you're older. This…" He paused and gestured out the window at the view of Kachemak Bay and the mountains across the water. "This is something else."

His comment brought her focus off of the ridiculous effect he had on her body. Marley's pondering about why Garrett was here danced in the edges of her thoughts. "Growing up here, sometimes I forget how amazing it is."

Garrett nodded slowly, took another swallow of coffee, and then changed the subject abruptly. "How do you like working at the lodge?"

Delia went with the shift in conversation. "I like it. A lot. I pretty much grew up there when your grandparents ran it and my mom worked there." She paused, wondering how much to share and then internally shrugged. She didn't have anything to hide. Her life was basically an open book in Diamond Creek. "Honestly, I didn't expect to end up doing exactly what my mom did, but it's what I needed.

I'm a single mom. The only thing that matters is making sure Nick has a stable life. I figure it's a bonus I actually like my job. Diamond Creek's a great place to raise kids and I love it. The plus side is your brother's a pretty good boss."

Garrett arched a brow at that and grinned. "Gage's a great guy. It sounds like the job's working out for you, which is good because I think he'd freak out if you weren't there. When he told us he was planning to come up here and open Last Frontier Lodge, I thought he was damn crazy. He's pulled it off though and with lots of thanks to you and your dad. At least that's what he says."

Delia couldn't help the warmth that filled her. Garrett's eyes held hers. The mood shifted, the air around them becoming heavy. Her breath became short again, her low belly clenched.

Garrett leaned forward, resting his elbows on the table. She lost herself in the blue blur of his eyes. His sensual mouth hooked up on one side. Uncertainty flickered in his gaze. He cleared his throat. "Look, about the other morning..."

She cut in. "No need to apologize. I'm sure you didn't mean..."

Garrett angled his head and shook it sharply. "Oh, I meant."

"You... What?"

He smiled ruefully. "I meant to kiss you. I'd like to kiss you again, in fact."

Delia's belly somersaulted, and her pulse went wild. Her mouth fell open. Flushing madly, she snapped it shut and bit her lip. "I, um, I guess I'm not sure what to say."

Garrett's gaze was pensive. "I'm not sure what I meant to say here. I just didn't want you to think it wasn't something I wanted." He took a gulp of coffee and pushed his chair back. "I told Gage I'd get back up there and help out with whatever he and your dad have going on today." He stood, his blue eyes boring into her. "I'll see you later, right?"

Delia nodded, still trying to absorb the last few moments. "I'll be in the kitchen for the rest of the day. Stop by for some cider when you guys get back in. It's windy out today, so stay warm."

He nodded quickly, his half-smile making her belly tighten and heat flood through her veins. With a quick lift of his coffee, he turned and left.

# CHAPTER 3

"*H*and me that wrench, would you?" Garrett asked Gage, holding his hand out from behind the heater.

He felt the cool metal land in his palm and quickly adjusted the fittings on the heater. He was pressed against the wall in the ski hut. He shimmied his way out from behind the heater and set the wrench on the floor. "That should do it." He swiped his elbow across his forehead, brushing his hair out of the way. "How did I end up being the one to do all the work?"

Gage glanced up and shrugged. "You forgot to tell me you learned how to install heaters. Don and I can get by, but you took care of it in half the time. Still can't figure out how you learned that in between all your court hearings."

Garrett leaned his head against the wall. "One of my buddies from law school grew up doing this kind of thing. I used to help out on weekends when he had extra work."

Gage adjusted the bindings on a pair of skis and propped them against the wall. He strode over to the heater and eyed the settings. "Safe to try it now?"

Garrett nodded. "Give it a go."

Gage turned it on. The small propane heater quietly started humming. Within moments, warm air began to filter out of the vents.

Gage threw a grin his way and took a few steps back to sit on one of the benches lining the walls. "Perfect. I promised Don we'd replace all the wood stoves in these little huts by the end of the winter. He's not gonna believe how fast we did this."

Garrett chuckled. "He was looking doubtful when we headed up here."

"Definitely. I think he was relieved you offered to help. He doesn't complain—ever—but working outside too much in the cold is hard on him. Thanks for offering."

"No problem. I figure I'd like to work as much as I can while I'm here." Garrett paused when emotion tightened in his chest and throat—reminding him why he wanted to keep busy. He didn't know what the hell was going on with him. Ever since he'd walked out of that courtroom days ago, he'd been out of sorts. Just talking to Gage about working on this place brought a wave of emotion through him. He didn't do emotion. He scrambled to pull himself together.

Gage watched him, his gaze curious. As discombobulated as Garrett was, Gage was probably the only person he could stand to be around when he felt the way he did. Gage was a rock, always had been. His support for his younger siblings was absolute. He'd been there through every step of Garrett's life, a quiet, steady presence. Garrett hadn't quite believed it when he heard Gage fell in love because Gage had always leaned in the direction of being a loner. But Marley was perfect for Gage. Garrett felt a sense of relief to know Gage's heart was in her hands.

"You okay?" Gage asked quietly.

Garrett shifted his feet under him and slid up along the wall before sitting down across from Gage. The small ski hut was warming with the heat circulating inside. The wind blew through the trees, sending snow in swirling flurries outside the window. He caught Gage's gray eyes. "Don't know. All the sudden I needed a break. Like I've never needed a break before in my life."

"I didn't know you ever took a break from anything. You're a workaholic. Sometimes I worried about you, but I figured you loved it. I mean, you worked your ass off to make your law practice what it is today. Did something happen?"

Garrett took a slow breath, staring out the window. The dark green spruce trees flexed in the wind. A sliver of the bay was visible, the water glinting under the bright sun. Clouds drifted across the sky. The view soothed him. That itself confused him. For so many years, he'd craved the hustle and bustle of work.

"I don't know what happened. I've been working so hard for so long, I hardly ever stop to think. Becca's been on me for years to slow down." He paused and shook his head. "Talk about pot and kettle. She's as bad as me."

Gage chuckled. "Well, you *are* twins. You two are different in some ways, but alike in many others. A relentless work ethic seems to run in the family though, so don't go beating yourself up for that."

"True. All I know is the other day I won a big case for an insurance company. I looked over at the woman who'd lost her lawsuit, and I could hardly get out of there fast enough. I had my assistant cancel everything for the next month and hopped on a plane. Sounds crazy, huh?"

Gage was silent for a long moment and then slowly shook his head. "Not to me. The details are different, but it's kinda what I felt like after I got assigned to desk duty. Years of being a Navy SEAL and then stuck on base. When Gram died, Last Frontier Lodge was all I could think about. Back to you though, what was the lawsuit about?"

"Huh?"

"The lawsuit? You said you looked at the woman who'd lost her lawsuit."

"Oh. Right. She sued my client, the insurance company, after they denied her son's claim for coverage after a car accident." His answer came out flat. A sense of unease rolled through him.

Gage's brows hitched and he angled his head to the side. "That makes sense."

"It does?"

"Yeah. Can't believe you didn't think of it. After you were in that car accident when you were little, mom and dad went through hell fighting with the insurance company over it. You were probably too little to remember all the details."

Garrett shook his head slowly. "All I remember is being in the hospital for weeks and then having to go through physical therapy forever. And that damn leg brace."

Gage was quiet again. When he spoke, his words were slow and deliberate. "You were six when it happened. Every night for weeks, mom slept in the hospital with you. She fought like crazy to get the hospital to let Becca stay there too." He paused and shook his head. "In the end, you were okay. While you were schlepping back and forth to physical therapy and wearing that damn leg brace, mom and dad were arguing with the insurance company. I don't know all the details, but I know they got something out of it, but not much. I said it makes sense because a case like that might hit a tad too close to home."

Garrett considered Gage's words, trying to assess his own recollections.

Gage spoke again. "Look, maybe it's none of my business, but you're my brother, so I figure it is. I'm proud of you. I thought you wanted this whole law thing, and you worked your ass off to make a name for yourself. But I've always wondered how long it would be before you wanted something else. It seems like you've been chasing the money when I don't think you really care about money all that much. For someone else, maybe that would be enough, but not for you."

Garrett thought maybe Gage's words should hurt, but they didn't. He was suddenly tired. He met Gage's eyes again. There was no judgment there, only concern. "I can see your point, but I'm about tapped out trying to process this right now."

Gage's nodded slowly. "No problem. Let's get back to the lodge."

After they packed up the tools, Garrett climbed onto a snowmobile beside Gage. "Bet I get there first," he said with a wave before he gunned the engine. They raced down the ski slope, wind whipping at them. They skidded to a stop beside each other at the base of the hill, well to the side of where the skiers came down. The swirl of snow made it impossible to tell who made it first. He walked with Gage toward the lodge. When they reached the door, Gage turned to him. "You canceled everything for the next month?"

"Yup. If it's okay with you, I'd like to stay here."

"You can stay as long as you'd like. I was thinking maybe we could get those heaters installed in every ski hut in the next few weeks. Can't do it without your help though. Whaddya think?"

"Sounds like a plan." Garrett couldn't help the tiny hum of pride he felt at being able to do something for his big brother. It wasn't much, but it was rare to find something he had more experience with than Gage. Those weekends in law school earning extra cash were turning out handy.

"Awesome!" Gage said with a grin as he pushed through the door into the ski lodge. They were entering through a side entrance into a hallway that led to the kitchen. There was a steady murmur of sound from the restaurant. Garrett had relocated to the spare bedroom in Gage and Marley's private quarters in the lodge. With the lodge mostly booked all the way through spring, he was relieved there was room for him somewhere.

He followed Gage into a utility room at the end of the hall. They kicked off their winter gear and washed up. Gage took off to find Marley. Garrett leaned his hands on the windowsill and looked outside. The ski slopes were dotted with people. Gage's quick observation about the potential effect that court case had on him was niggling in his brain. He had no memory of his parents fighting with the insurance company after his accident. He'd been a mere six years old when he'd been an unfortunate passenger in a car. He was riding in the back seat with a friend on the way to soccer practice. Another car plowed into them going through an intersection. Garrett had taken the brunt of the hit. Both of his legs were broken, along with many other injuries.

His memories of the accident itself were vague. His memories of waking up scared in the hospital were tinged with pain and confusion. What was clear in his mind were the hours of physical therapy and wearing a leg brace to school. He had been teased and taunted. He never played soccer again. He'd recovered fully and regained all of his strength, but he couldn't shake the odd fear about driving to practice. Instead, he'd thrown himself into studying and stumbled into the realization he was pretty damn good at academics. The driving force behind his desire to become a powerful lawyer was to never be the boy who couldn't fight back when he was teased. He'd turned to pick up games of basketball and running to stay in shape.

He couldn't quite believe that memories he didn't even know he had somehow affected him after he helped that insurance company fend off the lawsuit. As odd as it was, it made more sense than anything else. Garrett pushed away from the window and headed toward the kitchen. Delia had sauntered through his thoughts all day. He'd meant to tell her this morning that their kiss couldn't go anywhere. He was smooth at that with women—making sure they knew the boundaries. He'd opened his mouth and his well-worn script had failed him completely. Instead, he'd gone and told her he'd meant to kiss her and wanted to kiss her again. Rather than worrying about correcting himself, he was half relieved. Now, all he wanted was to find her and tug her into his arms again.

He pushed through the swinging door into the kitchen. Aromas of all varieties assailed him. The kitchen was bustling with activity. Garrett's eyes found Delia immediately. She stood by one of the waitresses and carefully adjusted the plates on a tray before holding the door for the waitress. Her honey blonde hair was pulled into a ponytail high atop her head. Loose curls framed her face. Garrett took the moment to simply look at her. He couldn't say what it was about her, but the sight of her knocked him right in the gut. He was accustomed to beautiful women and dated them in spades in Seattle. Delia was in her own category for him. She wore an apron over a wine red shirt. The apron hung so that her breasts curved above it, taut under her fitted t-shirt. His body responded instantly and she hadn't even noticed he was there.

He forced his eyes away from her. Now was most definitely not the time and place for him to get hard as a rock. The kitchen was filled with staff, all working toward the goal of keeping the food flowing into the busy lodge restaurant. He headed in the direction of the hot cider in the far corner. He opened the cabinet above to search out a mug when he felt Delia's presence. Without turning, he knew she was there. His body tightened at the feel of her warmth and the soft hint of vanilla she carried. He glanced over his shoulder. "Hey there. Hope it's okay I'm helping myself to some cider." He couldn't remember the last time he'd had to think about his expression, but he had to force himself to keep his eyes firmly on her face and his expression bland.

Delia held up a mug. "Thought you might need this," she offered with a small smile. Her cheeks were flushed, and her blue eyes bright.

"Just what I was looking for." He turned and accepted the mug from her before helping himself to the cider. He took a fortifying gulp and closed his eyes. When he opened them, hers were on him. "Perfect. I could live off this stuff."

She smiled again. In spite of the buzz of activity, the space around them quieted. It was as if they were alone. Garrett could see the flutter of her pulse in her neck. He wanted to lean over and lick the soft skin there. Her breasts rose and fell with a deep breath. Someone called her name, snapping him out of his trance. She turned, her ponytail swishing as she did. "Be right there," she called out. She swung back to him. When she bit her lip, a bolt of lust shot through him so hard he had to catch his breath. "I don't have much time to chat. Feel free to hang out if you'd like, but it's pretty crazy here for the next few hours. Gage keeps a corner booth in the back if you want to sit in the restaurant."

He nodded. "Right. I know you're working. I'll clear out and catch you later." He paused to top off his cider. Delia gave him a tiny wave and hurried off.

# CHAPTER 4

With a final wipe of the counter, Delia tossed the towel in the laundry bin in the corner and glanced around the kitchen. Another busy night was over. She leaned against the stainless steel table that ran lengthwise through the center of the kitchen. A loose curl fell across her eyes and she blew it away. She loved this time of night when the kitchen was quiet, such a contrast to the pace earlier. The window of light coming through the door into the restaurant darkened.

Harry, the supervisor for the floor staff poked his head through the swinging door. "Lights out. I'm the last one left, and I'm heading out. I'd better not hear you decided to stay late and bake again," he warned with a smile.

Delia grinned. "You have my word. I'm just checking on a few set ups for the morning, and I'll be right behind you."

Harry gave a quick wave before turning away. She listened to his footsteps become more distant as he made his way out of the restaurant. She remained still. The bright lights had been turned off, leaving the kitchen softly lit from a light in the corner and light spilling out from the office door. She mentally ran through what she needed ready before tomorrow morning when Garrett flickered in her thoughts. He'd practically taken up residence in her brain. About the only thing that kept him out of her mind was when she was too busy to think about anything beyond the task at hand. She recalled the moment earlier when she'd walked over to give him a mug for cider. It was as if they'd been in a bubble—of heat, of hot desire sliding through her veins, making her pulse run wild and her breath catch. She'd wanted to feel his lips on hers so badly, she'd almost forgotten they were in the middle of the kitchen with an entire roomful on observers.

Restless, she pushed away from the table and walked to the massive refrigerator. Swinging the heavy door open, she peered inside. Her staff had already left tidy trays of dough prepped for pastries in the morning. The hum of the refrigerator masked other sounds, so she felt rather than heard Garrett enter the kitchen. The hair on the back of her neck stood, a frisson of awareness racing up her spine. Her belly clenched and her breath became short. She carefully closed the door to the refrigerator and slowly turned.

Garrett leaned against the table behind her, his hands curled on its edge. Even in the dim light, the blue of his eyes was evident. His arms were muscled, curving into broad shoulders and a hard planed chest. Her hands itched to stroke up the lines of his muscles, to feel the strength of them around her. Her heart pounded so hard, it bordered on pain. She forced her eyes to his face. His glossy dark hair was rumpled. He wore a faded blue t-shirt and sweatpants. The angles of his face were shadowed. His sensual mouth, looking as if it was always on the verge of a teasing smile, hooked up at one corner. Somehow, when he smiled at Delia, she felt as if he must save those smiles only for her.

*Don't be silly. He's used to women falling all over him. He's a flirt and he's damn good at it. Don't fall for it. But maybe...* She swatted her hopelessly romantic thoughts away. Even though she knew better, there was a tiny corner of her mind that clung to pointless dreams—that someday the right man would come along and she'd learn what it felt like to be loved. It would be a man who loved her and didn't bat an eye at the fact she was a single mother. In fact, this dream man would love Nick as much as her and be the father he needed.

Garrett's voice cut through her mental wrangling. "Busy night, huh?"

"Always." Delia met his eyes and forced herself to hold his gaze. Which was hard because every second she looked at him, her pulse raced faster.

She stood a few feet away from him, and the space between them sparked to life. A flush spread through her body. She felt helpless against the tide of pure need cresting through her. A motion caught her eye, and she looked down to see his hand uncurl from the edge of the table and reach for her. He caught the loose tie of her apron and slowly tugged it. She couldn't have held still against his gentle tug if she'd wanted to. In two steps, she stood in front of him, the heat his body calling to hers. Liquid desire pooled in her center and dampened between her thighs. That was how desperately she wanted him—he hadn't laid a hand on her and she was slick with need.

In slow motion, he twirled her apron tie around his hand and tugged her another step closer. She could hardly hear for the roaring of blood in her ears. He slipped his hands around her waist, deftly untying her apron and tossing it on the table behind him.

"There. Now you're done for the night."

His words were soft. She could barely focus, but she noticed his pulse throbbing in his neck. The sight eased her, if only because she thought he might be half as affected as she was. She dared a glance at his eyes. The blue had darkened almost to navy. One of his hands had fallen to her hip after he'd tossed the apron away, the heat of it burning through the denim of her jeans. He lifted his other hand and slowly, oh so slowly, brought it up, brushing a loose curl away from her face and tucking it behind her ear. Her skin prickled in the path of his touch. A fine shudder ran through her when his thumb traced the edge of her ear and down along her neck, dusting over her racing pulse.

"I wanted...to do this earlier," he said, his words coming out raspy.

Before Delia could ask what he meant, he leaned forward and licked—*licked*—the soft skin of her neck right where her pulse beat. His startling touch, combined with the burning need she felt, elicited a long, low moan from her throat. If she'd been able to think rationally, she'd have been unable to recognize herself. He licked in a tortuous path down her neck and back up again, his lips nipping at her ear. She arched into his touch, her breath coming out in ragged gasps. He tugged her into his body, its hard planes serving to ratchet up the desire streaking through her.

His lips made their way to hers. He suddenly paused and whispered her name. Her eyelids were heavy, but she dragged them open to find his navy gaze on her. She saw a question in his eyes, but he was quiet. The moment was heavy with need and a driving sensation she'd never experienced. All she wanted was more. Thought didn't stand a chance against the depth of her sheer want for him.

Garrett's thumb coasted across the beat of her pulse, the soft strokes like flames on her skin. She could barely breathe. Every breath drew the need tighter in her core. Swiftly, he captured her lips in a bruising kiss. She opened instantly, her tongue tangling with his. His hand gripped her hip tightly and pulled her closer against his arousal, the hard heat of it pressing into her. Frantic, she flexed into him. She was hot, tight and achy, desperate to be closer, to find release. His hands moved over her roughly, one threading into her hair and freeing it from its loose knot while the other slipped up under her shirt. The rough, calloused skin of his palm struck sparks against the prickly heat of her skin. He stroked through her hair, fisting it in his hand as he tore his lips free from hers and dragged them down her neck.

She shoved her hands up under his shirt just as he flicked his thumb under the clasp of her bra and curled his hands around to cup her breasts. Another broken moan fell from her lips at the feel of his hands on her. Her nipples ached, so tight with need. His touch was rough and soft at once. He thumbed her nipples. Suddenly, there was a rush of motion as he tore her shirt off and she shoved his up. Hers floated to the ground, his following in seconds. She had a second to absorb his sculpted body, all hard muscle with a smattering of dark hair across his chest and narrowing down until the tempting trail disappeared into his waistband.

Garrett's breath hissed through his teeth before his lips closed around a nipple. Delia fell straight into the hot cauldron of need and sensation. He drew her nipple in between his teeth and tugged before dragging his mouth away to do the same to the other. Desire rushed through her. She couldn't get close enough, twisting herself against him. His knee slid between her thighs, the subtle pressure sending sharp spikes of pleasure through her. His lips made their way back up her neck to her mouth. Another deep, wet, drugging kiss, and she shifted restlessly against him. She dragged her hand up over the hard, hot length of him.

He took a step back and tore her jeans open, his hand slipping inside to stroke across the wet silk of her panties. He pulled back, his lips a whisper away from hers. He said her name, a soft command. She dragged her eyes open. Under the navy blur of his gaze, she was held tight in a rush of intimacy and sensation. He drew his finger back and forth across the drenched silk. Her breath fractured. She was so close, her pleasure spun higher and higher with each drag of his finger. When his name finally fell from her lips in a broken plea, he shoved the silk out of the way and delved into her folds. Need clawed at her as she arched into his touch. When he finally slid his fingers into her channel, she was so close to release, she began to throb around him. His touch was rough and swift, two deep strokes and she cried out, her climax rocking her.

When she finally drifted down, pleasure eddied through her. As consciousness began to sift through, Delia flushed, mortified she'd abandoned herself so completely. Though she barely had the nerve, she pulled her eyes up and found his waiting. She tried to remember the last time she'd ever had an orgasm with someone other than herself and couldn't. But Garrett had made her lose herself so easily. She didn't doubt he had far more experience that she did. An unplanned pregnancy and single motherhood didn't offer up much opportunity for sexual encounters.

The quiet hum of the refrigerator was distant to her ears. His hand slowly pulled out of her, coming to rest in the dip of her waist. She took a shaky breath and tried to marshal her composure. Her body hummed, tiny ripples of pleasure reverberating through her.

* * *

GARRETT COULDN'T LOOK AWAY from Delia. Her soft blue eyes looked as dazed as he felt. Kissing her completely shut off his brain and turned him into a foolish boy. He tried to remember the last time he'd been so overcome with need that he'd torn a woman's clothes off, desperate to touch her. He'd ripped her jeans open just to find out if she was as wet as he was hard. He approached seduction in a planned, organized manner—precisely as he approached everything in his life. With Delia, nothing made sense. He'd wandered down to the kitchen to see if there was any hot cider left, only to find her here by herself. One look at her, and it was as if she'd cast a spell on him. Not one single second of what happened had been planned. He'd been driven solely by the grip she had on him. Lust coiled tight inside every time she was near. She also reached through the walls around his heart, slipping through his defenses and eliciting tenderness and vulnerability.

In the usual course of events, he'd be expecting a woman to make sure his needs were taken care of right about now. Oh, he wasn't a selfish man and prided himself on making sure any woman he was with went away from the encounter satisfied. With Delia, her pleasure was indistinguishable from his. He wasn't kidding himself, he was so hard, he was on the verge of pain. Yet, all he'd wanted was to bring her release. Feeling her channel clench around his fingers and her body shudder against him had been the most intense and satisfying experience he could recall. He felt strangely exposed. He could feel her heartbeat against his chest, the rise and fall of her breath, her dewy skin against his.

He forced himself to take a breath, marshaling his composure. The man he was accustomed to being would say something sleek and gracious, offering an easy way to disengage. With Delia, his thoughts were fuzzy and all he could think was that he didn't want to move away. What he wanted was to lift her in his arms and carry her somewhere and simply be close to her. He scrambled for purchase in his mind. Her pulse fluttered in her neck, her hair fell in a loose tousle around her heart-shaped face, and her lips were kiss-swollen.

He cleared his throat. For the life of him, he didn't know what to say. As disoriented as he was, he also felt oddly comfortable with her. When he met her eyes again, uncertainty flickered there. He stroked a hand through her hair. As he was casting about to find something to say, she spoke.

"I, uh, got a little carried away there. I didn't mean…"

Garrett put his finger on her lips. He wasn't sure what else she meant to say, but he couldn't bear to let her feel embarrassed over any of this. He may have been lost and walking on ground foreign, but he knew what happened between them was special. "If you got carried away, then so did I. I might not have planned this, but I meant every second of it."

She sucked her breath in sharply, her cheeks flushing a deeper shade of pink. She nodded quickly. "So…?"

He thought quickly, considering where they could go. He glanced around, his eyes catching on the light spilling from the office. He started to slide his arm under her hip. She must have read his mind because she shook her head. "I have to get home. My dad's with Nick, but they're expecting me. It's not like…"

*Of course. Get a clue, Garrett. She's got a son. She can't just do whatever the hell you want. And you should be seriously wondering what you're thinking getting involved with her.* On the heels of that thought, he realized it didn't rattle him at all that she was a single mother. He'd grown up in a houseful of siblings and knew family was what mattered most. What rattled him was the depth of his attraction to her and the intimacy that wove between them so easily.

"Oh, right." He couldn't quite release her, but he eased his grip and took a breath. "Look, could we maybe, I don't know, have dinner? Or something?"

As soon as the words fumbled out of his mouth, he wondered if he'd completely lost his mind.

Delia bit her lip, instantly tightening the coil of lust inside of him. "Um, okay."

He went with it. He'd find time to get a hold of himself.

An actual date might get this insane lust out of his system. He'd be able to think, be able to be the man he usually was. "Just say when."

Her eyes widened. "Me?"

"Well, yeah. I don't have a schedule here. You do. You say when and I'll figure out the rest."

She bit her lip. Damn, she needed to stop doing that. He was barely getting a grip on his body, and every time she did that, his cock hardened. It didn't help she was still bare from the waist up. Her breasts were full and round with dusky pink nipples. A glimpse of red silk winked at him from where her jeans fell open. He knew what she felt like under there—hot, slick, and all lush, clenching softness. He forced his eyes back to her face. She was nodding. "Okay. I have two days off starting the day after tomorrow."

"Perfect. Tell me where to pick you up." He fumbled in his pocket and pulled his phone out. "What's your number?"

He punched it in when she recited it. Her eyes kept flicking to his, a mix of confusion and vulnerability. He wanted to wipe that look away, but he was too confused himself in the moment to know what to do about it. He coasted on the thread of his usual confidence he'd managed to latch onto. Though every cell in his body resisted, he took a step back and carefully slid her zipper up, savoring the soft give of her skin where one hand rested on her hip. Moments later, she'd covered her beautiful breasts underneath her shirt and was sifting her hands through her hair. He'd managed to get dressed and put himself back together. She walked into the office at the back of the kitchen and came out with her jacket on and her purse slung over her shoulder.

Haloed by the soft light from the office, she met his eyes. "I have to go." Her words fell quietly in the room.

"I'll walk you out."

When her eyes widened, he ignored her, along with the

sense of unease rising inside. She was perfectly capable of walking herself out, but he couldn't think straight. He followed her out into the cold, dark night. Stars glittered above, so close it felt as if he could reach up and touch them. Her car was running already. She stopped when she reached the door and looked up at him.

"Good night."

Her voice held that glimmer of uncertainty. He stepped closer and nudged her chin up with his knuckles. He caught her lips in a kiss and had to hang onto every ounce of restraint he had to keep the kiss brief. Her lips were so soft, so tempting.

"G'night. After tomorrow."

He waited while she closed the car door and drove away. The red taillights of her car became smaller as she wound down the curving driveway. The sound of her tires rolling on the road faded until he stood alone in the dark. He took a deep breath, the icy air a balm to his nerves. He turned slowly, pausing when he could see the moon over the mountains across the bay, its light shining in a rippling path on the water. A sense of peace fell over him as he stood there. It was so quiet he could hear the rustle of wind in the trees. An owl called softly. He took another breath and walked slowly inside, retracing his steps back into the kitchen. He made his way over to the corner where the hot cider was. He filled a mug and flicked the lights off on his way upstairs.

DELIA STOOD IN THE SHOWER, the hot water easing her tired body. Though she loved the hustle of busy days and nights at the restaurant, it meant long days on her feet. Tonight, she was weary and energized at once, riding the high from those mind-blowing moments in the kitchen with Garrett.

She couldn't have thought of a less sexy place, but now she'd probably blush the next time she walked by that table, recalling how she'd all but melted into a puddle under his touch.

Her body spun with ripples of sensations long dormant while her mind was a muddle. She considered just how crazy she was to let anything happen. Garrett needed to stay off limits for her. He was only here temporarily, and that wouldn't change. He had an entire life in Seattle, one far removed from Diamond Creek. She also didn't want him to think she was silly enough to be searching out a man who could be a father to Nick. She was proud of herself for rising to the occasion and raising Nick on her own terms. She wouldn't deny it would be nice to find love, but she was independent and liked it that way. Tonight had been an anomaly, a moment where her brain took a backseat to her body.

A tiny corner of her tried to speak up and point out that what she felt with Garrett went beyond purely physical. She ignored it. She couldn't let herself think too much about how it felt to be close to him. It was too dangerous. For a split second, she wondered if maybe she could go to Seattle, but she quickly nixed it. She loved her job and she was happy in Diamond Creek. She couldn't find a better place to raise Nick and would never be able to replicate the kind of support she had here from family and friends. Garrett would return to his life, and she would be nothing more than a memory. That's the way it needed to be.

She let the hot water wash away her day, taking the lingering sensation of his touch with it. After she climbed into bed though, her mind kept replaying those heated moments and her body hummed with the visceral memory of Garret's body against hers.

# CHAPTER 5

"*M*om!"

Delia whipped a brush through her hair and hurried down the hall, tying her hair in a loose knot as she came around the corner into the kitchen. She was getting ready to leave for work while Nick got ready for school.

"Mornin' Nick, what's up?" she asked as she dropped a kiss on the top of his head. He stood beside the bench by the door and was busy digging through his backpack.

Nick whipped his head up, his blue eyes wide. "I can't find my math homework!"

She met his worried gaze. "Where were you last night when you did your homework?"

Before Nick had a chance to reply, Delia's father came through the side door and tossed his gloves on the bench. "Started your car. Should be warm in a bit," he offered by way of greeting.

"Thanks, Dad."

Don nodded and kept walking, straight to the coffee pot. He poured a cup for himself and sat down at the kitchen table. Don was a loving father, but he was a man of action, not words. He wouldn't say anything sentimental, yet he'd start her car every morning and brush the snow off all winter long for her. She loved him for that.

Nick threw his backpack on the floor and sighed, leaning against the bench. Delia knelt beside him, stroking up and down his back. His shoulder blades felt like little wings under her palm. She could feel the shudder of his breath. She wished he hadn't inherited her tendency to worry. She knew he'd be beside himself until he found that homework, and if he didn't find it, he'd be on the verge of tears. He loved his first grade teacher, Miss Janie Stevens, known as Miss Janie to her beloved students. She was warm, witty, and practical. She also held her students to the standards she set and didn't coddle them, so Delia knew if Nick didn't find that homework, he would be marked down for it.

"Dad, you didn't happen to see Nick's math homework this morning, did you?"

She stood and looked over at him. Her father's weathered face, gray hair and warm blue eyes were a familiar, comforting sight.

He took a slow sip of coffee and cast his gaze on Nick. "Let's retrace your steps. Where were you when you did your homework last night?"

The next few minutes comprised Don patiently walking Nick through his night until Nick's eyes lit up. He went flying from the room, his feet pounding down the hallway. Moments later, he raced back into the kitchen, triumphantly waving several sheets of paper in his hand. "I left it in your study!" He threw his arms around his grandfather's waist and hurried over to his backpack, stuffing the papers inside. He was a conscientious boy, but not a tidy one. Delia figured she'd take conscientious over tidy any day.

Moments later, the bus had come and gone. Delia washed a few dishes and dried her hands, leaning her hips on the counter and glancing over at her father.

Don took another slow sip of coffee and cleared his throat. Her father wasn't one to hurry. "You know, it wouldn't hurt my feelings if you wanted your own place."

Her father's gentle comment elicited a mixed reaction. Sometimes, she desperately wanted to be living on her own. Yet, it was more what it represented than the actual reality she craved. She'd moved in with her parents after she had Nick out of necessity. While she wanted to be able to afford to take care of Nick and herself on her own, she loved her father dearly and was beyond grateful for the support he offered Nick.

"Dad, I…"

Don waved a hand and continued. "Hon, when you moved in with me and your mom after Nick was born, we were thrilled. I can't tell you how glad I am you were here to help when your mom got sick. The first few years after she died were hard and having you and Nick here made it easier on me. You've got a good job now. I don't want you feeling like I expect you to stay here. I'm no fool. I know you being here cuts into your social life, not because I think it should, but because you don't want to ask too much of me. Whether you're here or living on your own, I'll babysit whenever you need me to, so don't let that get in your way." Don paused for another swallow of coffee.

"Dad, it's not like I've been in a rush to move out. Being here isn't keeping me from a social life. I'm a single mother, I'm busy!" She heard the words leave her mouth and knew she was making excuses. The truth was she had let her life narrow to a small window because it was easier that way. She had friends, dear friends, Nick and her father, but she made no effort to even think about dating, or consider the idea of a relationship. Garrett challenged that, which terrified her. He kindled hopes and dreams she'd buried years ago while eliciting a desire she'd never thought possible. Her mind blinked back to the night before, and the very reason she'd left when she sensed he wanted to take things further.

To be fair, things were moving fast with him, faster than she was comfortable. She had no idea if anything she felt with him could go any further than mind blowing physical encounters, but it didn't change the reality she'd most likely hide inside the small room she'd created for her life. She took a breath and met her father's eyes. He saw so much. All he did was smile ruefully. "I know you're busy, hon. It's hard to watch you limit yourself. That's all."

At that, Don stood and nodded toward the door. "Car's probably warm by now."

She chuckled and grabbed her coat, throwing it over her shoulders. "Bye, Dad." She pecked him on the cheek and jogged out to her car. As promised, it was toasty warm inside.

When she got to work, she was quickly immersed in the busy pulse of the kitchen. Breakfast and dinner were the busiest times at the lodge. Lunch moved at more of a rolling pace since many guests were out skiing. When things slowed down enough for her to take a breather, she ducked into her office to go through the weekly supply order.

"Hey there."

Her head whipped up. Garrett leaned against the doorframe, his blue eyes locked onto her. A jolt of awareness rocked her and desire slid through her veins. *Delia, you are seriously a fool. All he did was show up, and your body's gone wild.* It was so bad, she couldn't do a thing to stop it. Her body had a mind of its own when it came to Garrett.

Her eyes coasted over him. She couldn't help but savor the sight of his muscled chest filling out his navy t-shirt. His jeans hung low on his hips. His sensual mouth hooked in a slow smile. Her breath hitched and her mouth went dry. It suddenly occurred to her she hadn't bothered to reply to him.

"Hey, um, how's it going?"

"Pretty good. I'm about to head out and help Gage install some heaters in the ski huts on the slopes. How are you?"

"Fine," she replied automatically. "My dad's glad you're helping Gage with those heaters."

Garrett nodded. "Heard the same from him."

She grinned. "He figured it would take Gage most of the winter on his own. Sounds like you might have some experience with it."

"So happens I used to do this for extra cash when I was in law school. My buddy's family owned a heating business. I helped out on the weekends," he explained with a small shrug.

"Why aren't you a helpful guy?" she offered, unable to resist the urge to tease.

Garrett held her gaze. The air around them hummed, a current sizzling to life. Her pulse raced, liquid heat built in her core.

His eyes darkened and his shoulders rose and fell with a breath. He took a step into the room, closing the door behind him. He moved so swiftly, she didn't have a chance to think. In a flash, he was at her side, leaning over. His lips caught hers in a searing kiss, his tongue sweeping inside. He pulled away just as swiftly. Her eyes slammed into his. He looked as stunned as she felt, which gave her a tiny degree of comfort.

He cleared his throat. "I can be pretty helpful…when I want." The corner of his mouth hooked in a small smile before he turned away. He opened the door and glanced over his shoulder. "See you tomorrow night."

She couldn't speak, so she simply nodded.

* * *

LATE THAT AFTERNOON, Garrett kicked the snow off his boots before stepping into the side hallway by the kitchen. He and Gage had installed two more heaters this afternoon. After heading upstairs for a quick shower, Garrett was about to return downstairs when his phone buzzed. Glancing at the screen, he saw it was his office assistant, Elaine Moss. Elaine had been with him since the beginning. Not only did he appreciate her relentless work ethic, but she was also one of the most practical people he'd ever known. He hesitated for a second before answering because he wasn't quite ready for reality to intrude. *What are you afraid of? Answer the damn phone.*

With a sharp shake of his head, he answered. "Hey Elaine, what's up?"

"I figured I'd better call you since you haven't called to check in yet and you haven't answered any of my emails." Elaine's tone was polite with a hint of frustration.

Garrett sighed and plunked down on the couch. Gage and Marley had a phenomenal view from their private quarters above the lodge restaurant. The ski slopes were in view with Kachemak Bay visible to the side. Snow was falling softly this afternoon, almost lazily floating down, the snowflakes plump and fluffy.

"I'm sorry, Elaine. I haven't been blowing you off on purpose. I know you're working overtime to cover for me, and I promise you'll be paid double for every extra hour you put in. I just needed a break. Truth be told, I haven't even checked my email."

Elaine was quiet for a moment. "I didn't think you were blowing me off on purpose. We're juggling a lot here with you gone. I've handed over your most pressing cases to Olivia Brooks. I know she's new here, but she's the only associate who has time to cover. She's doing a great job so far. Some of your old clients are getting pushy about when you'll be back. Even though I don't know why you're out, I'm telling them it's a family emergency. That's about the only thing that shuts people up. Should I start scheduling for you after the month is out?"

Garrett could feel Elaine's curiosity burning, but knew she was always gracious and would never push. He ran a hand through his hair, his eyes tracking a raven that flew by the windows. The sun was falling low in the sky, its soft light haloing the spruce trees. He took a breath. "I don't know, Elaine. I might be out more than a month. I'm sorry." His mind spun. He'd canceled everything for a month, but now that didn't seem even close to enough time for him to clear his head. Gage's comments about why that case got to him kept popping up, making him question if he even wanted to go back to what he'd been doing. That usually led to another round of questions, wondering if he was half out of his mind to walk away from the career he'd built. And then there was Delia—beautiful, sexy, sweet Delia who'd slipped through his sophisticated defenses. Hell, she was the only woman who'd made him notice he had defenses.

"I see," Elaine said quietly. He could sense her thinking and waited.

"Do you mind me asking what's going on? Out of nowhere, you had me cancel everything for a month, which is a long time in your world. Now it sounds like it might be longer. This isn't like you, Garrett."

"I know. I'm not trying to hide anything from you, Elaine. I haven't taken more than a few days off at a time since before I started law school. I just need a break. If I had a better explanation, I'd give it to you. I'd appreciate it if you kept this to yourself. As far as I'm concerned, have Olivia cover anything pressing and I'll check in once a week. Will that work?"

Elaine chuckled softly. "Garrett, did you forget you're

the boss? Of course, it's okay. Olivia will be fine. This is giving her a chance to prove herself right out of the gate. As far as I'm concerned, you deserve a break. How about I call you Monday after next in the morning?"

"That's more than a week away."

"Exactly. You don't need to check in any sooner than that. You're amazing at your job, but with Olivia's help, we can juggle everything we need. Take that break."

The line went dead in his ear before Garrett had a chance to reply. He slowly set the phone down on the table by the couch and sat in the quiet room. He watched the sun's slow bow behind the mountains, streamers of soft lavender and pink in its wake. In the fading light of dusk, he was startled out of his reverie when the door swung open.

Marley flicked the lights on and grinned when she saw him. "Hey Garrett! I didn't even know you were up here."

He stood from the couch and strode over to relieve her of the grocery bags dangling from her hands. Marley followed him into the kitchen area. Their private quarters were comprised of a wide room including the living room and a kitchen and dining area to one side with windows running the length of the room. A small hallway in the back led to the master bedroom and bath, along with two other bedrooms and a bathroom.

Garrett quickly got to work unloading the groceries. Marley giggled as she watched him. "Gage always said you were efficient. That appears to apply to everything."

He glanced up at her, meeting her warm green eyes. He shrugged. "Sorry. Didn't mean to take over like that."

Marley shrugged. "No worries. I'm not territorial about my kitchen. I was about to start dinner for you guys." She tugged a wine bottle out from the wine rack against the wall and arched a brow. "Wine or beer?"

"Beer. Can I help with anything?"

Marley shook her head. "Sit and keep me company. Gage will be up here soon. He was finishing up in the office."

Garrett took the beer Marley slid across the counter to him and sat down on a stool while she started dicing and sautéing vegetables.

"What's for dinner?"

"Stir fry. Hope you like it."

"I'll eat anything."

Marley's lips quirked in a smile. "You and Gage both." She lifted the cutting board to slide onions into a pan. "Can I be a little nosy?" she asked.

Garrett shrugged. "Sure. I showed up unannounced at your place with plans to stay for a month. I can't promise I'll answer all your questions. Hell, I might not even know the answers, but ask away." While Marley was new to the family, he trusted her completely. Once he'd seen her with Gage, any doubts he'd had dissipated. She was so clearly in love with his brother it made his heart twinge. Besides, she'd brought a lightness to Gage that Garrett hadn't seen since before Gage went into the military.

"What's up with you and Delia?"

Marley's question slammed into him. He didn't know what he'd expected her to ask, but it wasn't that. He thought he'd been careful about how he was around Delia in front of others.

"I can tell by the look on your face, I'm not crazy then."

"Damn, Marley. How about your give me a sec?" He knew his tone sounded slightly annoyed. He wasn't annoyed with her, but himself. He'd never been anything other than cool and slightly distant when it came to women. His life didn't leave much room for emotional entanglements, so he kept his relationships casual. They were more like business transactions. He had dates for premier work functions and not much else. He left women satisfied and made expectations very clear—there weren't to be any. He was so thrown off guard with Delia, he was fending off questions about what was going on with them when he didn't even know the answer himself.

He caught Marley's concerned gaze. "I didn't mean to push too far. It's just I noticed you go into her office the other day and saw her right after. She looked a little," Marley flushed and scrunched her nose. "Um, well, she looked like you'd just kissed her." She paused and looked at him carefully. "Delia's a good friend. I grew up with her, and her family was always close to mine. I know you don't know me that well, so I don't mean to be too pushy. It's just I don't want to see her get hurt."

Garrett nodded. "If I seemed annoyed, it wasn't with you. I, uh… Aw, hell, I don't know what to say. Look, I don't know what Gage has told you about me, but I work like crazy and relationships aren't really my thing. I'm not an asshole, but I get why you might be worried about Delia. I'd prefer if you didn't give Gage all the details because I don't want to piss him off, but the thing is I like Delia. I didn't plan on it. Just happened. So when you ask what's up with me and Delia, that's about all I can say."

"Okay." Marley eyed him for a long moment. "Seems like maybe I need to be worried about you too," she said softly.

Garrett's throat tightened, emotion washing through him. He forcibly cleared his throat. "Maybe so," he said with a soft chuckle.

Marley nodded and turned away to add some garlic, spices and sauce to the pan. She gracefully gave him a moment of space and quiet before she spoke again. "Do you want to talk about it? Gage has been worried about you, you know?"

Garrett nodded. "I know. He doesn't say much about it, but I can tell." He tried to think of a way to make sense of what was going on with him, but nothing did. He took a swallow of beer. "I'd love to talk about it if I thought I could make sense of what's going on with me."

Marley kept stirring and nodded as if she expected him to continue. So he did. "All I know is one day I couldn't even look at the woman who lost her lawsuit against the insurance company I was representing. That's the day I canceled everything and flew up here. My office assistant called today, and I can't even tell her when I'm going back because every time I try to think about it, I start to get a headache. Gage thinks I'm upset about that case because it hit too close to home."

She nodded. "He mentioned that to me."

He took a breath. "Right, so you know the details then. Maybe he has a point. I don't know. All I know is I don't even know if I want to go back anymore, and that makes me feel half crazy. I worked my ass off since the day I graduated from law school to get my practice where it is in Seattle. I make tons of money and have my pick of cases. It's what I thought I wanted and now I'm tired of it. Makes me fuckin' crazy."

Marley turned the burner off and took a sip of wine. "The details were different, but I went through something similar."

"The robbery?" he asked, referring to Marley's abrupt move back to Diamond Creek from Seattle after she'd been robbed and assaulted. With the help of a friend and former SEAL team member, Gage had been instrumental in finding justice for Marley.

"The robbery was the straw that broke the camel's back. I moved to Seattle with grand plans to start a tech company and be all kinds of amazing. I learned a lot and don't regret being there, but it didn't satisfy me the way I hoped. Sometimes you need to take a breather to find out what you want. The robbery gave me that chance. You're not me, but maybe you should stop worrying about answers right now.

From what Gage has told me, it's not like you can't afford not to work. I'm sure Gage already told you, but you're welcome to stay here as long as you need."

Garrett took a slow breath, the tension in his chest easing slightly. "Since I can't seem to find the answers, I'll try to take your advice."

The door swung open and Gage walked through. "Hey man," he said, slapping Garrett on the back as he walked by to drop a kiss on Marley's cheek.

Conversation moved on to lighter matters. Hours later, Garrett lay in bed, Delia lingering in his thoughts. Any moment he was alone, she was on his mind. And any moment she was on his mind, lust streaked through him. He was rock hard. He kicked the covers off and strode into the bathroom. His hand was nothing like what he hoped to experience with Delia, but the release was enough for him to fall asleep.

# CHAPTER 6

$\mathcal{D}$elia's phone chirped insistently. She came to a lurching stop in the parking lot and fumbled in her purse, not bothering to check the screen and see who was calling.

"Hello," she said quickly. There was a long enough pause that she repeated her greeting. After the next pause went a beat too long, she sighed and started to pull the phone away when she heard her name.

"Yes?"

"Delia, it's Terry."

Her stomach lurched and dread filled her followed with flashing anger. Terry was Nick's ever-absent father whom she hadn't seen or heard from since the week after she told him she was pregnant. At the time, she'd been in her senior year in college and believed herself in love with Terry. Or so she'd thought. She'd bitterly come to learn the man she thought she loved wasn't the man he was. She'd been in the untenable situation of only discovering she was pregnant when she was more than three months along. She'd been on the pill and rarely had her period anyway. She hadn't even blinked when she didn't have her period for three months straight. She'd been buried in classwork and working a full-time job at a local restaurant in Juneau.

After weeks of feeling nauseous every morning, her roommate, Sarah, had given her a long look and come home later that night with a pregnancy test. When Delia sputtered and told Sarah she was being ridiculous, Sarah had arched a brow and asked her if she'd forgotten to take her pills here and there. She'd missed a whopping total of two pills the month she'd gotten pregnant, but it was more than enough.

Delia remembered her last conversation with Terry more vividly than she'd like. Not because it was hazy with lost-love memories, but because it was the day she learned the sharp difference between perception and reality and came to learn how easily some people could lie. She swatted the memory away and focused on now. For a second, she tried to stay calm, but then decided it didn't matter. She'd never had her chance to let loose on Terry for leaving Nick to wonder who his father was and why he was never around. It would be hard for her to care less about Terry being a part of her life, but his absence mattered a lot to Nick, if only because it left a giant, gaping question mark in his heart.

"What the hell do you want, Terry?"

Silence greeted her, so she barreled onward. "It's been six years and you just pick up the phone and call? I don't know what you want or why the hell you've bothered to call now, but you'd better not think you can just waltz into our lives like this!" Her heart hammered, and she felt sick with anger.

"I, uh… Look, Delia, you have all kinds of reasons to be pissed off at me. I'm calling because my mom found out about your son and asked me to call you. She'd like a chance to meet him."

Delia noticed Terry didn't say "our son," but rather "your

son." She was alternately relieved and angry at the distinction. Her heart pounded, and her mind spun. All these years, she'd tried to come to terms with the fact that Nick's father had zero interest in him. She'd had to accept her own poor judgment and not beat herself up too much—incredibly difficult sometimes—and consider what she'd do if he ever reached out. She took a breath and tried to gather her composure.

Not yet. "Oh, so you think you can just call and ask if your mom can meet *my* son? You don't even have the nerve to say he's yours. I guess I should be thankful for that because you're nothing more than an accidental sperm donor." Her tone was bitter, and she didn't care. She had to cultivate her composure for Nick's sake, but not for Terry's.

Terry was silent for several beats. "Like I said, I get why you'd be pissed off. I'm only calling because of my mother."

Delia let his words sink in, her disappointment echoing against the absence of his interest in getting to know his son. She'd rehearsed imaginary answers to him a thousand times, but she hadn't rehearsed the answer to this. Nick's father wasn't interested in him, but his grandmother was. *Shit, shit, shit. Think, think, think.* Another deep breath, and she finally managed to speak. "The only reason I'm not hanging up the phone is because of *my* son. If your mom wants to meet Nick, she can call me directly. Feel free to give her my number. I'd rather you not call at all unless you're interested in a relationship with your son. If that ever happens, the terms will be mine. Are we clear?"

The last part she'd memorized, so the words slid off her tongue easily, even though fury was pounding through her. Her stomach felt hollow and her heart clenched with hurt for Nick. She waited.

Terry finally spoke. "I understand. I appreciate you're willing to talk to my mom. I don't think I ever mentioned her to you. Her name is Helen Carson."

"Nope. You never mentioned her to me," she replied, exasperated with him after only minutes of conversation.

"Right. I'll tell her she can call." After another awkward silence, Terry spoke again. "I get why you think I'm a total ass. I'm trying not to make things worse by trying to be something I don't know if I can be."

"What would that be?" Delia asked unable to keep her voice from vibrating with the force of her anger.

"A father. My life's been kind of a mess. I'm not the most stable guy. It may seem like I've been blowing you off all these years, but for the last few, I thought it was best if I stayed out of the way."

Questions tumbled through her mind, but she held her silence. It was up to him to do more than he had and she wasn't about to open a can of worms for Nick for someone who wasn't sure they were ready to be there for him.

"Okay. How about you have your mother call me? If something changes, maybe she can let me know."

"Right. Thanks, Delia."

"Sure." She ended the call without a goodbye. Her chest was tight and her throat ached and all of her pain was for Nick, her sweet little boy who raced at life with open arms, who asked questions about the father he'd never known and who accepted answers that were hard for anyone, much less a six year old boy. She leaned her forehead against the steering wheel and forced herself to breathe slowly and deeply.

After several moments, she sat up and glanced around her. She'd stopped to pick up mail at the post office. She opened the car door, letting the icy winter air wash over her. It settled her heightened nerves. Slamming the door behind her, she made her way inside, the thin layer of snow crunching under her boots. She quickly checked the mail and tucked it in her purse. On the way out, she was looking down when she heard her name. When her eyes lifted, they collided with Garrett. He stood near the end of the aisle where her post office box was, leaning against the wall. His jacket hung loose. He had one hand tucked in his pocket. It tugged his jeans down just enough to reveal a glimpse of his muscled abs. A curl of lust slid through her veins.

He arched a brow, his blue eyes teasing. "Do I get a hello?"

Too late, she realized she'd been silent for a beat too long. "Oh, right. Hello," she offered. More flustered than usual after her call with Terry, she couldn't think of what to say next.

Garrett saved her with a question. "So where are we going tonight?" His slow smile sent her belly somersaulting.

"I thought maybe we could go to the Boathouse. Have you been there before?"

He shook his head slowly. "I haven't been anywhere other than the lodge and Misty Mountain."

"It might not be like what you're used to in Seattle, but the Boathouse has some good food."

"Seattle leans toward trendy, but trendy doesn't always mean amazing food. Your cooking is as good as anything you could find in Seattle."

His quick compliment made her smile and then blush. He chuckled. "Don't tell me I'm the first person who's ever told you you're a damn good chef."

She shook her head rapidly. "No, but Diamond Creek's just a tiny corner of the world."

"Trust me, the big city's not all it's cracked up to be." His eyes, darkening to navy, coasted over her. Her breath became short and her pulse skittered.

"The Boathouse sounds perfect. Do you want me to pick you up?" he asked.

Taking her father at his word, she'd told him she was going out for the night with friends. She could have Garrett pick her up and not worry about too many questions. "Sounds good. Six o'clock?"

"You got it."

He pushed away from the wall and closed the distance between them. Before she could form a thought, he leaned over and nudged her chin up with his knuckles and kissed her. She was coming to learn that kisses with Garrett were dangerous. His lips caught hers, softly at first, shifting to rough and deep in seconds. His kisses wiped thought clean from her mind, sent sensations rolling through her hot and fast and made her melt inside and out. By the time he pulled away, she was practically a puddle. Her panties were soaked with desire and her nipples were so tight, they ached.

He held still, a fraction of space between their lips. "You make me crazy," he whispered roughly.

A laugh bubbled out of her and she nodded, flushing madly. He made her crazy too, but the second her brain kicked into gear, she had to remember to get a grip.

He nipped at her lip and then dropped another soft kiss before taking a deliberate step back. "See you at six," he said.

Someone came around the corner. Delia suddenly remembered where they were. That's how bad it was with Garrett. In the last few moments, it was as if they were alone in the world—nothing and no one existed but them and the desire shimmering in the air around them.

She glanced up and met his eyes, which held a hint of frustration as if it strained him to hold back. "See you then." She clutched the mail to her chest and walked past him, hurrying out to her car.

As she drove home, her mind bounced between anticipation about Garrett and the call from Terry. Just because Terry was a jerk didn't mean his parents were, but she didn't know them. By the time she considered trying to track them down, she realized she didn't know how to reach anyone in his family. She didn't even have names for his parents. Looking back, she felt a twinge of guilt, but she swatted it away. She couldn't be responsible for everything, especially when Terry had made it abundantly clear he wanted nothing to do with Nick.

She forced her mind off that worry and onto tonight. Even though part of her, a big part if she admitted it, was thrilled Garrett wanted to see her, another part of her was nearly frozen with fear. She hadn't been on a date since college. She had slammed the door shut on relationships for the last six years. It was overwhelming enough to have a baby on her own. Throw in the mix that her mother, whom she'd loved dearly, had been diagnosed with cancer and passed away within six months of the diagnosis, and Delia's emotional cup had been full. Once she thought her father was doing better, she'd just been hanging on and trying to find a steady job she could enjoy that paid the bills. Diamond Creek had a lot to offer in some ways, but most of the local restaurants were family owned. Gage's decision to reopen Last Frontier Lodge gave her an opportunity to do what she loved and paid well enough she could breathe easy for the first time in a long time.

Along came Garrett, an entirely unexpected curve in the road of her life. Oh, she'd fantasized about the right man coming along. She just hadn't figured he would be heart-stopping sexy and a high-flying, wealthy lawyer to boot. He was more the stuff of fantasy, and she wasn't so sure it was a good idea to indulge those fantasies. She reminded herself again and again, he wouldn't be here for long, and his life was in another world. Yet, she couldn't resist taking a shot to experience more of what she felt with him. Even if it hurt her in the end, she didn't want to go through life living small.

* * *

GARRETT LOOKED across the table at Delia. She was so damn beautiful. Her honeyed hair fell in tousled waves over her shoulders, framing her face with loose curls. Her blue eyes made him want to dive in and forget himself. He tried to recall if he'd ever had a dinner date that didn't involve business and came up with nothing. He only ever had dates to have a beautiful woman on his arm at business and social functions. Work ruled his life, including on the social plane.

Dinner with Delia had nothing to do with work. He was curious about her, a curiosity foreign to him. He wanted to *know* her. He was quickly coming to learn why she was so beloved to her friends and family. She was warm, kind, funny and went at life putting everyone else's needs ahead of her own. He admired the hell out of her for being a single parent. When the conversation offered an opening, he asked about Nick's father.

"If you don't mind me asking, is Nick's father from around here?"

Delia's eyes darkened, and she was quiet for a moment. "No, he's not. He's never been a part of Nick's life. It's an old story," she said with a shrug. "I got pregnant in college. It definitely wasn't planned, and that was the end of our relationship. I, uh, got pretty used to him not being around and honestly don't really want him to be a part of my life, but it matters to Nick. Oddly enough, he called me today. Right out of the blue."

Her words were matter of fact until the end. Cold anger coursed through Garret just thinking what it meant for her and Nick to have the man who was his father simply not be there. He wasn't sure what to say, but he felt he needed to say something. "I'm sorry. That, well, it sucks. Completely." He paused, gathering his thoughts. "What did he want when he called?"

She idly circled her wineglass in her hand, spinning the stem carefully. "He said his mother found out about Nick and wants to meet him. It took me so off guard, I didn't know what to think. I did get to tell him what an ass I thought he was though," she said with a bitter smile.

Garrett watched her carefully. She seemed open to talking. At a time when he would have usually tried to find a graceful way to exit the conversation, he found himself continuing. "I bet that felt good," he said with a wry smile.

She shrugged. "For a minute. Doesn't change anything for Nick though. Now I have to figure out what to do about Nick's grandmother."

Garrett nodded slowly, the first thought coming to his mind was how important his grandmother had been to him and his siblings. "What do you think you should do?"

"Probably let her meet him. Honestly, if it weren't for the fact that Terry *still* isn't interested in Nick, and I have to worry about whether she'll try to push that, it's an easy yes."

Garrett watched her, realizing that Delia just kept blowing him away. A situation in which anger easily could have overtaken her, she didn't deny she was angry, but she didn't let it color her choices. "Maybe you play it by ear and see what happens."

Delia smiled softly. "That's probably what I'll do." She took a swallow of wine and set her empty glass on the table. "Enough of the serious stuff, tell me some stories I can tease Gage about."

Conversation moved on to lighter matters. Not much later, their waiter approached the table with the check. Garrett quickly slid the tray into his hand, returning it with a credit card. Delia's hand paused in mid-air before she glared at him.

"You don't have to get that," she said, her eyes tinged with defiance.

"Maybe I don't have to, but I want to."

She bit her lip and her breath came out in a soft huff. His eyes locked onto her plump lips, sending blood shooting to his groin. He could barely keep a lid on the lust that surged through him whenever he was near Delia. His body rumbled on high idle, and all it took was a glance at the give of her lip under her teeth and his mind could focus only on how amazing her lips felt under his.

His eyes dipped down to the curves of her breasts. She wore a bright blue shirt with a scoop neck. The fitted cotton outlined her full breasts. Her skin, scattered with freckles, made his mouth water. All he wanted was to lean across the table and trace the soft curves with his tongue. He took a breath and forced his eyes up, only to notice her pulse fluttering in her neck. Another breath and his eyes collided with hers. His chest tightened, his body taut with need. He was not this man—this man who was half out of his mind with need for a woman and would do just about anything for her.

She flushed under his gaze, but he saw the answering desire in hers. She shrugged. "Fine then, but I get to return the favor."

He had to think for a second to recall what she meant. "Taking you out to dinner wasn't a favor. It's not like you need to keep an account so things are even."

He sensed a tension in her, but he wasn't going to take the bait.

Her breath huffed out again before she spoke. "I wasn't trying to make sure things were even, but I didn't want you to think I assumed you'd buy me dinner."

As off kilter as he felt with her, he realized she had her own reasons for not being certain of what things meant between them. "I didn't mean to assume. I just wanted to buy you dinner. That's all."

She bit her lip again. *Holy hell.* She needed to stop doing that. His reaction to her was beyond ridiculous. All she did was bite her lip a few times and he was ready to bend her over a table and sink inside of her. He was all about calculated pleasure, not this wild thrumming inside his body that he could hardly contain. He shifted in his seat, trying to will his erection away.

He was relieved when the waiter approached the table again. He quickly signed the credit card receipt and made small talk with the waiter for just long enough that he got his body under control. He stood and tugged on his jacket. Delia followed suit, and he was disappointed to see her curves disappear under her down jacket. He walked outside, his hand resting in the dip of her waist. A bracing wind cut across the parking lot. He savored the icy air. It took his mind off the relentless pulse of attraction coursing through him. He felt her shiver and wrapped his arm tighter around her. He couldn't help the wash of satisfaction he felt when she nestled closer to him.

He'd wisely used the remote starter for the truck he was borrowing from Gage. Once they were inside, Garrett didn't let himself stop and think. He glanced over at Delia. "How about we head back to the lodge?"

Delia held his eyes for a beat before nodding quickly. It started to snow on the drive back to the lodge. When he parked and went around to help her out, the snow fell softly around them. It was late enough that the outside lights had been dimmed. Stars winked in the black velvet sky, the moon coming in and out of view as clouds passed by. He was becoming accustomed to the odd sense of freedom and relief he experienced when he felt the deep quiet surround him here. A gust of wind blew Delia's hair wild. He caught her hand in his and led her to the door. Once inside, he immediately made his way to the kitchen. The restaurant was empty now and the staff hopefully gone. He'd become familiar with the schedule since he tended to be a night owl and often made forays to the kitchen for snacks and cider late at night.

A lamp remained on in the corner of the kitchen. With

Delia's hand in his, he headed straight for the corner where the hot cider waited. He'd come to savor her cider nightly—half because it was delicious with enough of a kick to take the edge off and half because he knew she made it. Without a word, he quickly filled two mugs and gestured toward the office. It crossed his mind that he'd never have considered what he was considering right now in another place or time. Without eliciting far more questions than he wanted to answer, there was no way for him to bring her up to Gage and Marley's apartment. He knew she lived with her father, so he'd immediately ruled out going to her place. His choice for their destination was the kitchen office, about the only private place he could think of.

Delia didn't appear to find the idea off-putting, which made him consider the fact that the women he usually dated would've flat refused to lounge on a couch in an office. It was Delia's office and held the same warmth she conveyed. It was decorated with a touch of whimsy with bright paintings of flowers on the walls, a multi-colored rug thrown over the hardwood floor, and a lamp with a stained glass shade on the desk. She flicked the lamp on and turned to him. The lust he'd been barely holding at bay surged through him. He kicked the door shut with his booted foot and closed the distance between them. He reached for the mug in her hands and set it on the desk, along with his. He lifted a hand and caught her zipper, slowly sliding it down. He held her gaze, giving her a chance to say something. Her lips parted and her tongue darted out to moisten them.

The coil of need tightened inside of him. He slid one hand inside her jacket, curling around her waist and tugging her close, as he stroked the other up her neck and into her hair. He finally gave in to what he'd wanted to do all night and caught her lips in a kiss. She opened instantly, inviting him inside, and he didn't wait. He threw himself into the kiss. She met every stroke of his tongue with hers. His pulse raced and waves of desire rushed through him. He slid his palm down from the dip of her waist to cup her luscious bottom and pulled her against his arousal, savoring her throaty moan.

He was anything but smooth and practiced over the next few minutes as he tore at her clothes. She was as frantic as he was, yanking his clothing off. His thoughts were a blur. He was driven solely by need. He glanced down to find Delia seated on her desk, her breasts rising and falling with her rapid breath. She was pure, seductive beauty, her eyes hazy with desire, her lips red and swollen, and her cheeks flushed pink. Her hair was rumpled. She was bare save for a pair of blue cotton panties. He stood in the cradle of her thighs, trying to catch his breath. His jacket and shirt were on the floor and his jeans were torn open. His cock was rock-hard and pulsing with every beat of his heart. Though he was consumed with need, when his eyes caught hers, his heart clenched.

# CHAPTER 7

*D*elia couldn't break away from Garrett's navy gaze, his eyes like hot embers on her. Her breath was ragged, and she was feverish with need. Garrett stood before her, his arms braced on the desk on either side of her. The sight of his bare chest sent her pulse up another notch. He was pure muscle, his arms bulging, his chest and abs etched from stone. Somewhere along the way in these heated moments, she'd torn his jeans open and shoved them down his hips. A pair of fitted black briefs didn't hide his bulging arousal.

The practical corner of her mind tried to assert itself. *Are you out of your mind? You're sitting here almost naked and about to have sex for the first time in six years, and you're not even thinking about stopping! Do you remember what happened last time you didn't bother to think?* As if she needed to be reminded. She didn't let herself think that way often, but the truth was Nick was the biggest blessing of her life despite coming from what she also considered her biggest mistake—a silly, childish brush with love that had been far from it. She'd been ruled by her practical side for so long now because she needed it.

But right now, in this moment, she didn't want to let her practical side make her decisions for her. If this turned out to be another mistake, at least it would feel amazing. She knew maybe it wasn't a good idea to let Garrett any closer, but the temptation was so strong. She didn't want to miss the chance to feel the way she felt with him. Even if he walked out of her life in a few weeks, and she had to shore up the walls around her heart in the aftermath. She already knew with certainty that the way she felt with Garrett when she managed to turn her brain off was something beyond anything she'd ever experienced. Even in the cloud of love-lust she felt for Terry all those years ago, the reality was the sex had been awkward and not particularly satisfying. The orgasm Garrett had so effortlessly brought her the other night was the first orgasm she'd had with anyone other than herself.

Holding Garrett's gaze, she placed her palm on his chest and stroked it slowly down. His breath hissed through his teeth when she slipped her hand into his briefs. She thrilled to his low groan when she curled her hand around his heated length. His eyes still on hers and his breathing rough, he circled her lips with his thumb before he traced a path down between her breasts. Her nipples contracted and her belly clenched as his touch traveled over the curve of her belly and stroked across her cotton panties. He stroked softly once or twice, and her breath broke on a moan. She was already drenched with desire. She shifted restlessly into his touch. He abruptly stepped back, tugging her hips to the edge of the desk.

He moved swiftly. In one motion, he pushed her panties out of the way and leaned forward and brought his mouth against her. Her hands fell away from him and she hung onto the edge of the desk, frantically grasping for something to anchor her as fierce sensation overtook her. His fingers joined his mouth, plunging into her channel and stroking as he licked through her folds. Her hips rocked into his mouth as he teased around and over her clit. She lost all sense of anything other than the pressure gathering and spinning inside until it spun loose, releasing wave after wave of sharp pleasure.

Garrett eased the stroke of his fingers and stilled his mouth before slowly pulling back. His lips trailed upward on her body in a leisurely path. He paused to tease her breasts, licking around a nipple before closing his lips over it. Heat twisted inside of her. Still reeling from the reverberations of her climax, she arched into his touch. His mouth traversed to her other breast. Pleasure streaked through her when he bit down quickly on her nipple before arching away. He fumbled in the pocket of his jeans, yanking a condom out and tearing its packet open. Frantic to feel him inside of her, she attempted to help him roll it on, which led to a collision between her forehead and his chin.

"Ow!"

"You okay?" he asked, brushing the hair out of her face, his eyes snagging on hers.

"I'm fine." Her voice was breathy.

Garrett caught her mouth in a kiss, a sensuous tangle of lips and tongue. She felt his cock nudge between her folds and couldn't hold back her whimper. He pulled back, just far enough she could feel his lips move against hers. *"Delia."*

Her eyelids were weighted, but she forced them open to the blur of his blue gaze. He threaded his hand in her hair, sliding it around to cup the back of her head. Shivers of need rippled through her as he slowly rocked his hips against hers, creating a delicious friction as he slid through her drenched folds. He coaxed her closer and closer to the edge. She flexed into him, desperate to feel him fill her.

*"Garrett, please..."*

He answered her plea with his body and smoothly surged inside of her. Her slick channel throbbed around him. She savored the fullness, the depth of his strokes. He set a steady pace, the push and pull of his cock sending pleasure ricocheting through her. She struggled to get closer, twisting against him in response to the need coiling tighter and tighter inside of her. Every stroke of him inside of her brought her closer to the delicious edge she chased. One hand gripping her hip, he loosened the other in her hair and slid it down her body, bringing his thumb against the center of her desire. A deep surge and she convulsed around him. He followed her over the edge, her name falling from his lips in a hoarse cry as he drummed his hips into hers. His forehead fell to the curve of her shoulder.

* * *

ONCE GARRETT MANAGED to catch his breath, he curled his hands under Delia's hips and lifted her against him.

"Where...?"

"Shower," he replied, taking the few steps into the tiny bathroom off her office, which contained a small shower.

He eased her down once they were in the bathroom. After tossing his condom in the trash, he tugged her into the shower with him. It was a first for him to want to linger like this after sex. He wanted anything to prolong his time with her. When he turned off the water, she lifted her eyes to his, her lashes spiky with moisture. His chest tightened. He was caught in entirely unfamiliar territory. He had no experience with the intimacy he felt with Delia. Though he'd felt it the first time he kissed her, he'd half convinced himself all he needed to do was get her out of his system. Instead, after finally feeling the clench of her around him, all he wanted was more. The more went beyond physical desire to an emotional need he didn't recognize.

Her eyes held a question, but he was too focused on trying to manage the emotions tumbling through him to find words. Instead, he caught her lips in a kiss and grabbed a towel. After they dressed, they found their way into the kitchen. Garrett, who hadn't enjoyed a late night snack with anyone since he was a boy, found himself laughing while Delia shared stories of slumber parties at the lodge during the slow months. She sat cross-legged on the stainless steel table, her damp curls framing her face. He didn't want the night to end, so he lifted her in his arms later and fell asleep on the couch in the office with her tucked close against him.

# CHAPTER 8

*G*arrett adjusted the fitting on the heater he and Gage were installing and pushed out from behind it. He leaned against the wall and rolled his shoulder. It was tight from his cramped position behind the heater.

"Should be good to go. How many more of these do we have?" Garrett asked.

Gage glanced over from where he was adjusting the settings on the front of the heater. "Only three left. Between fumbling my way through and trying to fit it in between everything else, I figured it'd take me all month to get these done. With you here, we'll be done a lot faster." He leaned back on his heels when the heater started to hum and warm air began to sift from the vents. "Perfect."

Gage stood and snagged the toolbox as he sat down on the bench. He started putting tools away. Garrett silently handed over the tools by the heater.

"Any idea how long you plan on staying?" Gage asked.

Such a simple question and one Garrett should be able

to answer. Yet, he couldn't. He must have been quiet a beat too long because Gage looked over, his gray eyes concerned.

Garrett cleared his throat. "I don't know. If you need me to clear out, all you have to do is say so."

Gage shook his head. "You can stay as long as you like. You wanna talk about it?"

Garrett pondered how to explain that every time he thought about going back to Seattle, back to work, he simply couldn't stomach it. He kept dodging his own thoughts about it because he was completely confused. He met his brother's eyes and shrugged. "Don't know that talking would help. Ever since I walked out of court that day, I just... Hell, I don't know. I keep telling myself I need to go back. I mean, I have a law firm to run! Here I am, trying to screw my head on straight and doing a shitty job of it."

Gage was quiet for a long moment. "Maybe you're not."

"Not what?"

"Not doing a shitty job of it. It depends on how you look at it. If it's to get back to Seattle and the life you led there, then maybe so. If it's to give yourself a little time to figure out if you'd like to do something else with your life, then maybe you're doing exactly what you need to do."

Garrett nodded slowly. "Okay then. Any idea how long I should give myself? 'Cause right now, I feel like I'm casting about in the dark."

Gage flashed a grin. "You always did love a deadline. Hate to tell you, but you might have to let that go for this."

Garrett rolled his eyes. "Great, just great."

"Since it looks like you'll be around for a bit, why don't you move into one of the lodge suites?"

Garrett started to protest, but Gage cut him off. "Don't go thinking we mind having you, but I know you're used to having your own space. One of the suites will be available after tonight. I told Harry to keep it open for you."

"You don't need to give up bookings for me."

"Consider it a selfish move. You getting away from the treadmill of your job and Seattle is the best thing that's happened to you in years as far as I'm concerned. I figure the chances of you sticking around are better if you're not shacked up in a tiny spare bedroom. Don't worry about bookings. The lodge is doing far better than I ever expected for its first winter."

"I'm damn proud of what you've done with this place by the way."

Gage's return smile was wide. "Took a lot of work, but it's worth it." His eyes sobered again. "I'm guessing you're gonna tell me to shut the hell up, but I have to ask. What's up with you and Delia?"

Garrett's mind flashed to Delia's bare body, her legs curled around his waist as he thrust inside of her. He didn't quite think that's what Gage had in mind, so he took a breath and tried to think of a better answer.

"Okay, so I guessed right," Gage said, his tone one of resignation.

"You guessed what?"

"I'm not blind, and I'm your brother, so I know you better than I'd like sometimes. I guessed you had a thing for her, and I can tell by the look on your face that you do." Gage paused, his eyes considering. "I know you're not an asshole and you wouldn't purposefully hurt her. Delia has a heart of gold. I've never asked, but far as I can tell, she hasn't been involved with anyone for years. She's too busy being a single mom and working. Don't consider anything with her if you're after a fling. She's not that kind of woman. Don would love for Delia to find someone, but he would definitely be upset to see her get her heart broken by my big-city brother."

Garrett ran a hand through his hair and eyed Gage. "I'm not going to break her heart."

Gage considered him and nodded. "I know you wouldn't plan on it."

"Does anyone plan something like that?" Garrett asked sarcastically.

"Look, I'm not trying to tell you what to do. Delia would be furious if she knew I said anything to you. For all I know, she's not the least bit interested, but my gut tells me she is. Just keep in mind she's not like the women you date in Seattle."

Garrett felt a twinge of chagrin. "Didn't mean to be an ass. You didn't need to tell me Delia's not like the women I usually date. While I can't make many promises, I can promise the last thing I want to do is hurt her." Emotion knotted in his chest and throat. He leaned his head against the wall and took a slow breath. "Ah, hell. I'm in way over my head with her, if you're wondering."

Gage's eyes softened. "What do you mean?"

"If I could explain, I would. Just that she drives me half out of my mind. It's not something I've had much experience with, that's for sure."

Gage chuckled softly. "Starting to wonder if I need to be as worried about you as Delia."

Garrett shook his head and pushed himself up from the wall. "Nah, I'll be okay. Let's get back to the lodge."

Gage didn't push the topic of Delia further and accepted Garrett's abrupt end to the conversation. Much to Garrett's relief because Garrett found talking about Delia disconcerting. Thinking about her was like riding on a boat in a storm —tossed and buffeted by the waves of emotion she elicited.

*  *  *

DELIA WALKED into Sally's where she was meeting Marley and Ginger for lunch. Sally's was a fixture in Diamond Creek, a restaurant and bar housed in an old renovated barn. The kitchen was situated in the center of the structure with the bar on one side and a restaurant with booths lining the walls and long tables in the center. Evenings were busy here, but lunches tended to be quieter. Delia veered to the restaurant side and made her way to the booth where Marley and Ginger were already waiting.

"Hey there. Sorry I'm a few minutes behind. Nick forgot his backpack, so I had to double back." Delia hung her jacket on the corner of the booth and sat down beside Marley.

Ginger glanced up from the menu and smiled, her blue eyes crinkling. "I barely beat you here. How's it going?"

"Busy, as usual. You?"

Ginger shrugged, her shiny brown hair falling off her shoulder. "Same, same."

Marley turned to Delia. "Harry was totally freaking out this morning. He says too many things go wrong when you're off."

Delia shook her head. "What now?"

Marley tucked her auburn hair behind her ears and shrugged. "Something about the breakfast buffet. That's all I know."

Their waitress arrived to take their drink order. When she left to get their drinks, Delia leaned back and listened to the back and forth between her friends. Along with Marley, Ginger Sanders was an old childhood friend. Ginger was outspoken, feisty and funny. When Marley called Delia this morning about getting together for lunch, Delia figured the timing was perfect. She needed some blunt advice, and she could count on Ginger for that. Marley would counter Ginger's occasionally harsh observations with her softer touch and wry warmth.

While hearing Ginger's latest grievances about trying to date in Diamond Creek, Marley glanced slyly at Delia. "Well, I think Delia might be interested in someone."

Delia flushed instantly. Ginger swung to her, her eyes narrowing. "What are you keeping from me?"

"Nothing!"

Marley angled her head to the side and arched a brow. "Really?"

"Oh, all right. There might be something with Garrett."

"You mean Gage's brother, the super hot and sexy lawyer? Spill it," Ginger demanded.

Still flushing, Delia took a breath and considered what to say. Where to start when she'd jumped from no dating and no sex for six years straight to the hottest, most mind-blowing sex she'd ever had? Just thinking about it, her pulse quickened and her blood heated.

"Wow, I'd guess there's more than nothing going on," Ginger said wryly.

Delia glared at her. "Cut it out. I don't know what to say. Garrett and I..." She shrugged. "We had dinner last night. I don't know that it means much of anything to him. He's only here for the month. I figured I might as well since if I ever plan to try having a relationship again, I'd better get some practice at dating."

"Sounds like he'll be here more than a month," Marley offered.

Delia's heart pounded and hope unfurled its wings. *Don't be silly. You know there's a time limit to anything with him, so don't get your hopes up for anything else.* Her practical mind quickly asserted itself, but it had little power over her body and her emotional state. She glanced at Marley. "What do you mean?"

Marley leaned back as their waitress arrived. Delia impatiently waited through the delay of having their food served. Once the waitress walked away, Marley replied. "Gage said he talked to Garrett yesterday, and Garrett doesn't know when he'll go back to Seattle. Gage set him up in one of the suites for now. He's hoping Garrett will change gears and maybe get out of Seattle."

Delia couldn't snuff her questions. Her curiosity about Garrett was almost constant. By the end of lunch, she'd learned that Gage had been worried about Garrett working too hard for years and he'd never thought Garrett could be satisfied with his career as it was. The more she got to know him, the more she could see why Gage would wonder. The surface of Garrett's life was of wealthy lawyer who catered to corporate interests. Yet, the man she was coming to know was down to earth and caring.

"You think he'd want to leave Seattle?" Delia asked.

Marley took a swallow of water and angled her head to the side. "You realize you probably know Garrett better than I do by this point," she offered with a grin.

Delia flushed and shrugged.

Marley continued. "Gage thinks Garrett might be better off if he got out of the rat race. If he stays in Seattle, it'll be hard for him to do that."

"What do you think?" Ginger asked, archly.

Delia twisted a lock of hair around her finger. "I don't know him that well yet, but I can't see him being happy just doing the corporate law thing. I bet he's really good at it, but it seems like he'd, I don't know, want more."

"So you're saying corporate lawyers are shallow, then?" Ginger asked with a sly grin.

"No! I'm saying it doesn't seem like he's satisfied with that. As for moving away from Seattle, that's another thing altogether. I'm not sure what to think about that." She fought her blush, but it was impossible. Speaking aloud about the hopes and dreams that she kept trying to shove away brought her feelings too close to the surface.

Ginger caught Delia's eyes with another grin. "Well, if you were planning to play it cool, you blew it."

Delia grinned and shook her head. "You know I'm

terrible at playing it cool." She paused, considering the other issue she'd hoped to discuss with her friends. "On that note, I need some feedback, and it's not such a fun topic."

At Marley and Ginger's simultaneous nod, Delia continued. "Terry called the other day."

"What the hell? What did he say?" Ginger demanded.

Marley's questions were right on the heels of Ginger's. "Are you serious? What did he want?"

Delia held her hands up. "He was calling because his mother found out about Nick and wants to meet him. I told him he could give her my number, but now I'm freaking out. I have no idea what to say if she calls. Should I let her meet Nick?"

Ginger leaned back and set her fork down. "Damn. They don't give you instructions for this kind of thing." She glanced in Marley's direction and back to Delia. "Short answer: yes. Long answer: when the time is right. You've never even met her, right?"

Delia shook her head. "Never. Terry and I dated in college for maybe four or five months. It wasn't like I brought him home to meet my parents, or vice versa."

"In the long run, if Nick has a chance to get to know his grandparents, that's a good thing. It's the kind of question where you have to think ahead. How would Nick feel if he found out later he had this chance and you refused to let him have it?" Marley asked.

"I know. Even though it's hard because Terry hasn't been there—at all—I would never want to keep Nick from anyone in his family. It's more how to go about it."

"So does Terry want to meet Nick?" Ginger asked.

Delia shook her head slowly. "He didn't ask. He did say he hasn't been too stable and didn't want to try to be something he couldn't. I suppose I should appreciate that, but it's not easy. Not because I want to have to deal with him, but because of how it affects Nick. He used to ask about his dad more often. Now it's only once in a blue moon."

"It makes me mad for Nick, but it's better for Terry to be honest," Marley said.

"I know. It doesn't change anything for Nick though."

"No, but at least he called when his mother asked to meet Nick. He could've blown her off," Marley commented.

Delia nodded. "I know. For that, the only thing I can think is to start with a few calls and go from there. I'm sure she's going to want to meet Nick right off, but I don't think I'll be comfortable until I have a chance to get to know her a little.

Ginger nodded vehemently. "She'll have to understand that. If she doesn't, that tells you a lot right there."

Delia left a while later, considering she'd thought she'd needed her friends' help around how to deal with the call out of the blue from Terry, but in the end they'd merely validated what she already thought. She would have to wait to hear from Terry's mother and go from there. As for Garrett, hearing that he might stay beyond a month only left her stirred up inside. Her foolish hopes danced inside— her mind was having a more and more difficult time keeping her heart quiet.

# CHAPTER 9

The following afternoon, Delia was up to her elbows in dough when Nick came racing into the kitchen. He skidded past her and tossed his backpack on the couch in her office.

"Slow down, Nick!" she called.

Nick spent afternoons at the lodge once school was out, just as she had done when her mother ran the kitchen here so many years ago. Gage's flexibility about scheduling and his easy attitude around allowing children to be at the lodge when needed made her job worlds easier. She and several other staff had children who were dropped off by the bus after school. They took turns keeping an eye on them.

Nick had started to run back out of her office and shifted to a walk in response to her admonition. He made his way to her side, hugging her waist before stepping away to glance up at her. "What's for snacks today?"

"Apple slices and peanut butter." She lifted a hand away from the dough she was kneading and gestured to a small platter in the corner of the kitchen.

Late morning and mid-afternoon were the slowest times

in the restaurant, so she usually prepped a few snacks for Nick and the other children. He instantly left her side and helped himself. While Nick was busy chewing, Don came through the swinging door from the back hallway and ruffled Nick's hair.

"Hey bud, how was school today?"

Nick launched into a summary of his day for his grandfather, chomping noisily on his apples in between words. Delia finished kneading the dough and transferred it to an oiled bowl. Wiping her hands on her apron, she was in mid-conversation with one of the line cooks when Garrett and Gage walked into the kitchen. Her belly fluttered and her pulse kicked into gear. Gage went straight for the massive refrigerator, grabbed a bottle of juice and tossed one over to Garrett who caught it easily. He leaned against the counter by Don and Nick and started casually chatting with them.

"Delia?" Lyle, the line cook she'd been talking with, asked.

She realized she'd stopped talking mid-sentence when she'd been discussing the specials with Lyle. Flustered, she glanced back to Lyle. He arched a brow, his eyes moving beyond her to Garrett and back again. "Think I've got it for tonight. We'll do the maple-glazed salmon with asparagus in addition to the other specials. Will that work?"

She nodded and turned away, wishing like hell she wasn't prone to blushing. It had been bad enough whenever Garrett was anywhere near before, but after he'd all but set her on fire the other night, heat surged through her at the mere sight of him. His eyes snagged on hers. It was as if he flicked a flame to life, the current between them sizzling from all the way across the room. Her breath hitched, and her mouth went dry. She forced herself to breathe slowly. They had an audience and she couldn't show how weak-kneed and dreamy she felt.

Garrett's eyes held hers for a hot moment before he

glanced to Don, replying to something Don said. Delia busied herself wiping down the counter where she'd been preparing bread. Conversation flowed around her. She managed to get her breath back under control, but her pulse hummed. She jumped when her father called her name.

"Okay if Nick goes with Garrett and Gage to do some repair work up on the slopes?" Don asked.

Nick was bouncing on his heels. He loved any chance he could get to ride on the snowmobile up the slopes.

Gage caught her eyes. "He won't be out of our sight. We're doing some work on one of the ski huts and taking a look at the lift where it's been getting hung up on the turn."

"Of course he can go." She walked over and knelt down in front of Nick. "Put your coat and gloves on before you head out and listen to them," she said sternly. Nick nodded vigorously. She knew Gage and Garrett would keep eyes on him, but she didn't want him to accidentally get in their way.

When she stood up, she found herself a hair too close to Garrett. Her blood heated at the feel of his presence. She couldn't keep from looking his way and collided with his gaze. His eyes darkened. The air around them compressed. She had to force herself to remember they were in a room full of people.

Nick broke the moment when he raced into her office, coming out with his jacket swinging in the air. "When can we go?" he asked, skidding to a stop at Garrett's side.

Garrett grinned and ruffled Nick's hair. Delia didn't realize how, but in the short time Garrett had been here, Nick already looked up to him the way he did Gage. Her heart clenched. He had a good male role model with her dad, but she knew he wanted more. He soaked up attention from Garrett and Gage like a sponge. Watching Garrett with Nick pulled all sorts of strings in her heart. He was easy-going and comfortable with Nick and with the other kids around the lodge. He'd make a great father. She'd trained herself never to hope for that for Nick, but it was hard not to with Garrett. On the heels of that thought, it was as if a knife twisted in her gut. A fresh wave of anger toward Terry rose inside. His damn call the other day brought long-buried feelings to the surface. She hadn't realized how much she wished Nick had a father who was actually involved in his life. She shook her head sharply and knocked her mind off that loop. She watched as Nick followed Garrett and Gage out to the deck. Garrett helped Nick get situated on one of the snowmobiles before he climbed on in front of him. The snow kicked up in a swirl behind them when Garrett drove off behind Gage.

* * *

"HAND ME THAT WRENCH," Garrett said.

Garrett felt the cool metal of the wrench in his outstretched palm. He glanced up at Nick whose bright blue eyes, so similar to Delia's, were watching avidly. They were seated against the wall on opposite sides of the propane heater they were installing. Garrett handed the wrench Gage had just put in his hand to Nick. "Okay, now we need to tighten the fittings." He pointed to the two fittings. "Hold the wrench like this," he paused and put it in place in Nick's hands. "Let it do the work for you." He watched while Nick started to turn the wrench. He lost his grip for a moment, but tightened his hand and gradually circled the wrench.

When the wrench stopped turning, Nick looked up, a question in his eyes. Garrett reached over and gave the wrench a firm push. "Perfect. Now do the same thing on the next one."

While Nick carefully finished, Garrett thought back to what Marley had shared about Nick's absent father—namely that he'd never been involved in Nick's life in any way. Cold anger knotted in his chest whenever he thought about what that meant for Delia and Nick. She'd gotten by on her own. He couldn't help but wonder what it would be like if she didn't have the support of her father. Delia stood out in so many ways for him, but the fact she was a parent was yet another factor that should have given him pause. But it didn't. The only answer to the puzzle of why was because it was Delia. In the usual course of events, he kept his life emotionally uncluttered. But then, he'd yet to encounter a woman who pulled so strong and hard on his emotions that he could hardly think straight.

He found his heart softening in every interaction with Nick and his mind envisioning how he could provide the support to Delia that she'd never had. He'd like to tell himself it was just money, but that was the least of it. For crying out loud, he pictured himself teaching Nick every-thing from how to install a heater to practicing his pitches with him. *Dude, you don't even know if he plays baseball. So what? I'm sure he plays some sport. Did you forget you don't even live here? You have a whole life in another state.*

Garrett caught himself about to shake his head at his internal dialogue and sighed. He knew he had to deal with his life soon, but he was finding it harder and harder to think about being too far away from Delia. Without an ounce of guile, she'd slipped through the cracks in his defenses when he hadn't even known he had them. He forced his attention to the moment when Nick said his name.

"Yup, looks good. Let me check it." Garrett reached over and gave the wrench a good turn and handed it back to Nick. "Usually Gage does the honors, but why don't you turn it on and give it a test run?"

Gage caught Garrett's eyes and grinned. He'd busied himself replacing the caulk around the two small windows in the hut. By the end of the month, all of these warming huts would have brand new highly efficient propane heaters and would be snug and comfy for skiers who got too cold or injured and needed to wait for the emergency team.

Nick scrambled out from behind the heater. Garrett pushed himself up and stepped over to the bench to sit down. Nick stood stock still in front of the heater, his eyes darting back and forth. He finally looked over at Garrett. "Which button do I push?"

"The big green one."

Nick turned back to the heater and slowly pushed his finger against the green button. "It works!" he exclaimed as the heater started to hum. He held his hands in front of the vent. "It's warm!"

Gage chuckled and stepped away from the window to kneel beside Nick. "You helped make it work. Good job." He held his hand up for a high five. Nick slapped Gage's hand enthusiastically and raced to Garrett. At the sound of the slap when Nick's small palm collided with his, Garrett's throat knotted with a wash of emotion. Hell, he was in deep.

A while later after they'd returned to the lodge, his phone rang. He walked into the small efficiency kitchen in his suite, snagging his phone off the counter.

"Garrett here."

"Elaine here," Garrett's assistance parroted. "Sorry to call you ahead of schedule, but I figured I'd better call you before Tom Carlton does."

Tom Carlton was a regular client. He ran Carlton Industries, a corporate conglomerate that included ownership of the insurance company Garrett had represented in multiple lawsuits. He'd succeeded in getting every single one thrown out. Garrett charged his highest rate to Carlton Industries, in part because Carlton was notoriously difficult to deal with. He had trouble keeping attorneys as a result of his pushy, demanding nature. A part of Garrett's personality thrived on managing clients like Carlton. He had little patience for bad behavior and often ignored demands if there wasn't an active case. He made no apologies.

He sighed. "What's he in a snit about now? We don't have an active case with them right now."

"Since when did that stop him from being a pain in the ass?" Elaine asked wryly.

Garrett chuckled. "Never. Anyway, what's he want now?"

"He has a new case for us. Another insurance one."

"Give it to Olivia. She can handle all of those going forward."

He'd never enjoyed working insurance cases and was happy to let Olivia hone her skills on them. Problem was, he knew damn well Carlton wouldn't like it. Carlton had an inflated sense of importance and tended to think it was beneath him to work with associate lawyers.

"I'll call him myself."

"Thanks for volunteering," Elaine replied. "You know if he doesn't hear it from you, he'll raise a stink."

"You think Olivia can handle him?"

"She'll be fine. He's all bark and no bite. I'll give her the rundown. How about you let me know once you've talked to him?"

"Of course." He glanced at the clock above the stove. "I'll call first thing tomorrow morning. He gets crankier towards the end of the day."

He hung up to the sound of Elaine laughing. He walked to the windows and pushed the curtains back. The suite was situated on the corner of the lodge and offered a view of the slopes with the bay in the distance. The sun was setting behind the mountains. Even though Alaska's days were short in the winter, he didn't find it bothersome. He was so accustomed to the gray days of Seattle that early sunsets offered more color. Rays of faded gold reached into the sky from behind the mountains. Lavender and pink wove through the gold and shimmered on the water below. He leaned his shoulder against the window frame and let the quiet soak through him. He watched the sunset almost every evening here. For the life of him, he couldn't remember when he last took time to watch the sunset before he came to Alaska.

Calling Carlton was an annoyance. It should have motivated Garrett to make some sense of what he was doing. He'd put his life on pause and didn't know precisely why. He shoved away from the window and snatched his phone up, calling the only person he could think to call. After two rings, his twin sister answered.

"Hey Garrett, I was wondering when you'd call. Are you in withdrawal yet?" Becca asked.

Garrett could see her sly grin. Becca was two minutes older than him. She'd only stopped lording that detail over him a few years ago. He and Becca had always been close, and she knew him like no other. After a childhood of pushing and pulling at each other, they'd gone to law school together. Becca followed her passion to advocate for those who didn't have a voice and was currently a prosecutor who specialized in cases involving victims of abuse. Garrett had followed the money and was damn good at arguing just about any case handed to him.

"Hey Becca, how's life in Seattle and what the hell do you mean by withdrawal?"

"Busy, busy. You haven't rubbed elbows with enough money since you took off, so I figured you'd be stressing out about that. I know you can afford not to work with what you charge, but a month off? That's strange for you."

Garrett plunked down on the couch. "No withdrawal. That's kinda why I called."

Becca's tone softened. "You okay?"

He took a breath and gathered himself. "I'm fine. I'm just

confused. I figured it was time to call you since I can't seem to think my way out of this."

"What are you talking about?"

"All I know is the day I left, I couldn't get out of the courtroom fast enough. I figured I just needed a vacation, but now that I'm here, every time I think about going back to work, I couldn't give a shit." He paused. When Becca didn't say anything, he continued. "You remember much about my accident?"

"Of course. I probably remember it better than you. I begged mom to let me stay at the hospital. She finally worked it out so I could stay a few nights there. You had your legs in stationary casts. When you finally got home, I helped you learn how to walk with your brace. Don't you remember practicing in the hallway?"

He had vague memories of walking painfully back and forth in the hallway, but he didn't specifically recall he'd been practicing with his leg brace. "Kinda. Gage thinks I got freaked out about my last case because mom and dad had to fight with the insurance company after my accident. Know anything about that?"

"Back up a sec. What do you mean you got freaked out about your last case?"

"It was a lawsuit against a health insurance company. I won the case and when I was on my way out of the court-room, I couldn't even look at the woman who lost. Usually, I go over and make nice, but I couldn't." He shifted uncomfortably. It was a small thing really. Yet, it bothered him nonetheless.

"Oh." Becca's tone was soft, but it spoke volumes. She'd railed at him after law school when he set up his practice and went after corporate clients. She'd told him he was wasting his talents. Over the years since, she'd kept quiet, but he knew she was disappointed in him. Becca loved a cause and corporations weren't a cause to her. She thought they abused their influence and clogged up the legal system.

After a quiet moment, she continued. "Gage was right. Mom and dad had to fight like crazy to get your surgeries covered. I don't remember all the details, but it had something to do with the fact that the driver who caused the accident was uninsured. Their insurance company didn't want to pony up. I'm pretty sure they got most of it covered in the end, but it wasn't easy. Maybe that had something to do with how you felt. I said it way back when you started the whole corporate law gig, it's not your personality. You actually have a heart, Garrett. The money's nice and all, but I figured you'd reach a point when it wasn't enough. I think you managed to stay with it as long as you have because you were so driven to be the best. Now that you're sitting pretty with your pick of clients, there's nothing to drive you anymore. You can't tell me you care about what happens to your clients. Every time I hear about one of your cases in the news, it's because you beat back some lawsuit. I didn't ride you about that before because I wanted to give you a hard time, but because I didn't see how you could stay interested over the long run."

He listened to Becca's words and leaned his head against the back of the couch. "Maybe you were right."

"I didn't say it because I wanted to be right. It's because I know you. I can't see you doing what I do because that's too gritty for you, but maybe you should branch out, take some non-profit cases, do some pro bono work, and see how that feels."

Simply considering something other than facing off in court when the point of his argument was merely to win felt good. He took a breath. "What would you say if I told you I'm thinking about staying up here for a bit?"

"I'd say a change of pace might be the best thing that's happened to you in years."

Becca could be blunt to the point of harsh, but she was also one of the kindest people Garrett knew. While she would be the first to share her opinion about his career choices, she wouldn't bother to gloat when he changed gears.

"Well, I'll keep you posted. No final decisions right now, but I'm not confirming a timetable when I'll return to work. Tell me what's up with you?"

Their conversation moved on with Becca filling him in on her latest dating fiasco. He hung up the phone several minutes later and stared out at the gathering darkness.

Delia was working tonight. He'd texted her earlier asking if she minded if he stopped by her office after the restaurant closed down. She'd replied with a smiley face, which he took to mean yes. He was starting to get used to it, but it still startled him that all he had to do was think of Delia and his body tightened with anticipation. Joining the almost constant state of arousal she evoked was the disconcerting depth of feeling that came along with it—an unfamiliar ache in his heart, a wash of protectiveness, and a sense of uncertainty. An uncertainty born from the hopes she kindled in his heart, hopes he hadn't even known he could have.

# CHAPTER 10

*D*elia re-read the text message from Garrett earlier and wondered when he'd be coming by her office. The last of the kitchen staff had left a few minutes ago. She'd told her father she would be working late for pastry prep. She sensed that he suspected something else might be up, but he didn't push. She was restless. After another few moments, she decided to take matters into her own hands. She'd checked the computer room assignments and knew which suite Garrett was occupying. Moving quietly through the halls, she made her way upstairs and knocked quietly on his door.

She heard muffled footsteps on the carpet before the door swung open. Garrett stood before her in nothing but a towel, his skin still damp from what must have been a shower only moments ago. The shadowed light emphasized his muscled chest and arms. She itched to touch him, to feel the strength of him under her hands. Heat suffused her. His eyes widened before he stepped back and gestured for her to come in.

"I was about to head downstairs," he said, his voice gruff.

She nodded and walked over to the windows. She needed to get a hold of herself. She'd never felt such an intense draw before. What she felt was more than physical with Garrett, but her body was so unaccustomed to the depth of need she experienced with him that it overtook her. She glanced around the small suite. She'd seen these rooms many times. The main room contained a king-size bed with a small couch and chairs beyond the foot of the bed. The kitchen efficiency was to the other side with a small round table for dining. Windows ran the length of the room. She peered outside at the velvety night sky. Stars were scattered across the sky like diamonds, sharp in the clear winter air.

She felt Garrett come up behind her and rest his hands on her shoulders. His hands slid down her arms, the heat of his touch sifting through her thin cotton blouse. Her pulse quickened as his lips landed on her neck, his kisses lighting small fires under the surface of her skin. Her arms fell loose as she arched into him. One hand threaded into her air, gently tugging her head back, exposing her neck. He blazed a sizzling trail along her neck. His other hand slid around her waist, caressing the curve of her belly and rising up. Filaments of heat seared through her everywhere he touched. He began to unbutton her blouse, slowly, one button at a time, his fingers stroking each inch of skin revealed. He flicked the clasp of her bra undone on his way down. Her nipples tightened unbearably. By the time her blouse fell open and he slipped the straps of her bra off her shoulders, her breath came in pants.

Her sex clenched, drenched with desire. Garrett's hands cupped her breasts, his light touch notching her need higher and higher. She was hot and achy, her skin feverish and damp. She arched her hips into his arousal, savoring the groan that fell from his lips. His cock was hard and hot. She turned swiftly and yanked at his towel. It fell easily.

*"Delia...not now..."*

*"Oh no. Now."*

She might be years out of practice, but she'd already picked up that Garrett liked to direct the action. For the most part, that was perfectly fine with her, and oh was he ever the master at directing as he'd left her boneless and sated after every encounter. But for now, she wanted a taste of him and to bring him pleasure, so she intended to take charge.

She knelt in front of him and stroked a finger up from the base of his cock to the tip, her tongue following suit, before closing her mouth around him and drawing him inside. His body was taut as his hips arched into her. She set to exploring every inch of him with her mouth, licking, sucking and stroking. She curled her fist around him, stroking his shaft in her wet grip. His breathing became more ragged and broken moans fell from his throat. He tried to tug her up, but she ignored him, drawing him deeply into her mouth one last time until she felt his cock throb and pulse. She pulled back to watch him, stroking him in her palm. He jerked, cum spilling onto her breasts. A wave of satisfaction rolled through her to see him so. His eyes opened, his gaze heavy and dark.

"That wasn't supposed to happen so fast," he said, frustration marking his features.

Delia stood slowly. "Yes, it was," she said, feeling saucy. She didn't recognize this side of herself because she'd never experienced it. She thrilled to the feeling and arched a brow.

Garrett shook his head and moved swiftly. In seconds, he'd torn off her jeans, thrown them to the floor, and lifted her in his arms. He strode into the bathroom, nudging the light with his shoulder. After reaching into the shower to turn it on, he carried her in with him. The shower in this suite had been updated and had a rainfall showerhead in the center of the ceiling and blue glass tiling. He adjusted her weight, and she shifted in response, curling her legs around his hips.

Time blurred as he backed her up against the wall and slowly slid her down until her bottom rested on the seat in the corner. Hot water poured down around them as his palms slid up her calves and pushed her knees apart. His mouth came against her. Her head fell back against the cool tiles as sensation washed over her in waves. He explored her folds with his tongue, teased over and around her clit and stroked his fingers deeply inside. Pleasure built and built until she thought she would explode. He abruptly pulled back and lifted her. She heard the tear of foil and felt him roll the condom on. In one swift motion, he sank into her. Her channel clenched around him. She clawed at his back, flexing into him as he pushed her against the wall. He surged into her again and again, his motions rough and unmeasured. She clung to him, chasing the sweet release. In one driving thrust, pleasure burst through her and she cried out. He found his release with another surge, a hoarse cry falling from his lips.

Awareness filtered in as the hot water sluiced over them. Garrett's strong arms held her without pause. He lifted his head, his eyes meeting hers through the steam. He slowly eased his grip and pulled away from her.

* * *

GARRETT'S PHONE buzzed on the nightstand and he rolled over to check it. Delia was tucked close against his side. All he wanted was to stay right where he was. Delia's soft body was warm in her sleep. He'd promised he'd wake her, so she could drive home. Rationally, he completely understood she couldn't spend too many nights away, but it didn't change the fact he wanted more than stolen hours with her. He rolled back over and soaked in the feel of her. She shifted, her voice gravelly with sleep when she spoke.

"Was that the alarm?"

"Mmmhmm." He nuzzled her neck and stroked down her body from her shoulder over the lush curve of her breast, into the dip of her waist and coming to rest on her hip.

She rolled in his arms. "I have to go."

"Don't want you to."

She giggled. "I don't want to go either, but I need to be there in the morning."

He took a breath. "I know." He dropped a kiss on her neck and kicked the covers away.

She sat up, rubbing her eyes and then climbed out of bed. She quickly got dressed, and he followed suit.

"You don't need to get up with me."

"I'll walk you out. Do you have a remote start?"

She looked at him for a moment before nodding. He didn't want to explain how he felt—the curl of protectiveness, the need to make sure she was okay.

She nodded toward the counter as she walked to the bathroom. He grabbed her keys and hit the remote start button. Several moments later, he walked at her side through the long hallway and down the curving staircase to the reception area.

The wind had picked up during the night. An icy gust whipped at them when they stepped outside. He slid his arm across her shoulders and tugged her to his side. The snow packed ground muted their footsteps on the walk across the parking lot. When they reached her car, Delia tilted her head up.

"Oooh, look!"

She pointed. He followed her gesture and saw green and blue shimmering in the dark sky. His breath caught. The northern lights were rare, even in Alaska. In the quiet with nothing other than the soft hum of her car's engine, he watched the colors flutter in the sky. It was as if a sheer curtain of green and blue was waving in the breeze. He stood still, stunned into silence.

After several moments, Delia's voice broke through his trance. "Amazing, huh?"

He took a breath, the bracing air soothing him. "Yeah. I've never seen the northern lights."

"Most people haven't," she replied softly. "I should get going."

He tore his eyes away from the sky and looked down at her. "Right." He reached around her and opened her car door. "See you tomorrow." He caught her lips in a quick kiss before stepping back. She climbed in her car and drove away.

He stood alone in the dark after she was gone and watched the northern lights dance in the sky, the blur of blue and green alive in the night.

Only when he shivered in the cold did he walk back inside. He glanced at the clock as he lay down in bed. One in the morning and he was wide awake, his mind spinning over thoughts of Delia and what to do about his life in Seattle. More and more, he wanted to shift the gears in his life, but it confused him how he could so easily give up what he'd built. Not to mention he wasn't certain if the draw to Alaska was mostly Delia. He worried he was about to make major changes because of a woman, something he'd promised himself he would never do. What if he uprooted himself and his fantasies about Delia didn't bear out? What if he couldn't be the kind of man she deserved? That last question tore at him.

# CHAPTER 11

*D*elia hung her apron on the hook by her office door and closed the door behind her. End of the month reports were due, and she needed quiet for that. The kitchen hummed with the activity of prepping and cooking. The crew had just finished the breakfast rotation and was capitalizing on the temporary lull in the restaurant to get ready to serve lunch. She sat down at her desk with a sigh. Her mind wandered to Garrett, or rather her mind replayed the loop in her brain—the feel of Garrett's lips on her neck, hot water running over her as he pounded into her, falling asleep in his arms, and walking outside into the icy cold, intimacy weaving between them as they stared up at the inky black sky dancing with northern lights.

She shook her head sharply and tapped her keyboard. Her laptop powered up. She quickly opened up the accounts and got to work. A while later, she rubbed her eyes and leaned back in her chair. She emailed the reports to Gage and the lodge accountant before standing to look out the window. Last Frontier Lodge was situated at the base of several peaks and afforded views from almost every window. The slice of view from her small office was of the thick spruce forest and a mountain ridge in the distance. Snow dusted the evergreen trees. An eagle screeched in the distance, its call sharp and unmistakable. She watched and waited before the eagle lifted from the trees, spreading its wings wide. With an average wingspan of six to seven and a half feet, eagles were immense birds. The eagle lifted in flight slowly before swooping in a half circle and flying above the slopes.

Delia's phone chirped. She slipped it out of her pocket and answered without glancing to see who it was.

"Hello."

There was a long enough pause that she remembered she might be getting a call from Nick's grandmother.

"I'm trying to reach Delia," a woman said politely.

"You found her," Delia replied, her heart beating rapidly.

"Delia, this is Helen Carson. Terry gave me your number and said it would be okay if I called you."

Delia took a deep breath. "Yes, Terry told me you wanted to call." She didn't really know what else to say. This was an awkward introduction and loaded with emotional baggage for her. It brought up her lingering anger with Terry for so thoroughly shutting the door on Nick, along with her anger at herself for being so foolish. She didn't regret having Nick, not even for a second, but she regretted her inability to see Terry for who he was. If she'd had more sense at the time, perhaps Nick would have a father who cared.

Helen spoke again. "I'm sure this is awkward for you, and I'm sorry for that. Terry never told me about you or about Nick. If he'd told me, I'd have reached out much sooner."

Delia's chest loosened slightly at Helen's words. "Awkward is one way to put it. I'm not really sure how to go about this."

"Me neither. I was furious when Terry first told me a

few months ago, but I knew right away I wanted to find a way to talk to you. My husband passed away four years ago, and it breaks my heart he never knew he had a grandson. I'm not sure how much you know about Terry, but things have been difficult with him. Him finally talking to you about me is the best thing he's done in years. I gave him time to talk to you first, but told him if he didn't, I'd track you down myself. I'm assuming since you gave permission for him to give me your number that you're open to the possibility of having Nick meet me." Helen's voice lilted toward the end and then broke on a soft sob.

Delia realized she was nodding, but Helen couldn't see her. She stepped away from the window and sat back down at her desk, needing the chair underneath her. "You guessed right. To be honest, I didn't know what to think when Terry called. He hasn't been in touch at all. Since he made it clear he wasn't interested in being involved in Nick's life, I didn't go out of my way to find him."

Long silences seemed to be the norm in this uncomfortable conversation. Helen broke the silence. "Can you tell me a little about Nick?"

Delia took a breath and did something that was incredibly easy—bragging about her son. Mothers often had to curb that tendency, as it could be annoying to some. For once, Delia had the chance to talk as long as she wanted about all the good things about Nick. At some point, there was a knock at the door and Harry, the floor supervisor, poked his head into her office. When he saw she was on the phone, he nodded quickly and waved her off when she started to stand.

"Excuse me Helen. I'm at work and I need to check on something. Hang on a sec." She moved the phone away and called Harry's name. He leaned back into her office.

"Do you need me?" she asked.

"Take your time, but the hostess tonight called out sick.

We could use a little help up front if you get a chance."

"I'll be out in a few minutes. Let me finish my call and change."

Harry was already on his way out. His voice floated behind him. "Thank you!"

When she brought the phone back to her ear, Helen spoke. "It sounds like you need to go. Would it be possible for you and I to meet sometime soon? I don't know if there's a right way to do this, but if I were you, I'd want to meet me first."

Delia recalled Ginger's comment that if Helen didn't understand the need to move slowly, it would tell Delia a lot about her. Though she didn't have much to go on, Helen at least had enough sense to acknowledge the strangeness of this situation, along with the necessary patience to take it one step at a time.

"Sounds good to me. I'm not sure how we'll do that though. I don't even know where you live."

"I live in Anchorage. Terry's father used to work for the legislature for many years, so we were often back and forth between Juneau and Anchorage. After he died, I stayed in Anchorage. I'd be happy to drive down to Diamond Creek. It's been years since I've been there, but it's a lovely little town. We used to go fishing there sometimes in the summer."

Delia processed that information and took another breath. Getting through this call was starting to seem like the easy part. Meeting Helen, finding a way to talk to Nick about her and eventually introducing them were the bigger challenges. "In that case, when do you think you could come down for the day?"

Several moments later, she hung up the phone. Restless, she walked to the window again. The sun was bright against the white snow. She turned away quickly. She didn't have time to dwell on this. No matter what, it couldn't be bad to follow this through with Helen. She couldn't fathom keeping her from Nick, so she'd have to take it one step at a time. If it turned out that she wasn't a good influence for Nick, at least Delia would have given her a chance.

Delia walked to the small closet and tugged out some spare clothing she kept there. She spent most of her time in the kitchen, but occasionally worked out front for larger events and for situations such as now. She quickly changed into a fitted black skirt that hugged her hips and widened to a fluttery twirl at her knees. She topped that with a simple white blouse. Pausing in front of the bathroom mirror, she freed her hair from its ponytail and brushed it loose around her shoulders. She removed the smudges of flour in her hair and on her face. After a swipe of pink lip-gloss, she stepped into a pair of simple black heels and considered herself presentable.

The late afternoon and evening passed in a blur. Guests coming off the slopes piled into the restaurant, along with local residents. From early evening on, the restaurant was at capacity. Returning from escorting a family to their table, she looked up to find Garrett waiting by the entrance. He hadn't seen her yet, so she had a moment to observe him unnoticed. His elbow rested on the reception stand, and he idly flipped a pen in his fingers. His rich brown hair tended to be just past the edge of tidy, as if he ran his hand through it often. He wore soft, faded jeans and a navy cotton jersey shirt. His muscled chest was outlined under his shirt. Her pulse quickened just thinking about the feel of his body against hers.

She considered that the way she saw him probably wasn't the way he usually was. The man she'd heard him to be before she met him was different—at least in her imagination. He was a wealthy corporate lawyer in Seattle. He probably wore suits every day and night. His hair might still be mussed, but she doubted it. When she'd hoped to eventually find a man, she'd never considered a man such as Garrett. For starters, he likely had his pick of women in Seattle. If she'd met him in his world, he'd have intimidated her so much, she couldn't even imagine talking to him. Yet here in Diamond Creek, he wasn't what she expected. She knew Gage and had met the rest of his family, so she knew he had loving parents and a close family that tended toward boisterous. She'd pictured a sharp, cold man when she'd heard about Garrett. Instead she found a warm, funny, strong, dark and sexy man—one who took her breath away and pushed her body to stratospheres of pleasure she'd never known existed.

Garrett turned his head, a slow smile spreading across his face when he saw her standing in the archway between the reception area and restaurant. She walked over to the desk, her heels clicking on the floor. When she reached his side, he whistled so softly, no one but her could hear it. Heat suffused her, a whole body blush racing through her.

GARRETT WATCHED Delia walk toward him. She wore a black skirt that hugged her lush bottom and flared around her knees, accentuating the dip and curve of her waist. Her fitted white blouse was simple, yet the tease of her skin in the vee at the top and the way her breasts strained against the fabric heated his blood. He shifted on his feet. Now was definitely not the time and place to look like a foolish teenage boy with a hard on. When it came to Delia though, he felt like a foolish boy most of the time. When she reached his side, he couldn't stop himself from giving a soft whistle. Her cheeks pinkened. He resisted the urge to tug her close for a kiss. They were far from alone, and she was working.

Her heels tapped on the floor as she walked behind the desk. He toyed with the pen on the reservation list. Her hair fell forward as she leaned over. Her blue eyes lifted to his. His brain went soft. All he could think about was how her lips would feel under his. They were soft, pink and full. He flipped the pen back and forth, trying to corral the lust racing through him. She arched a brow and cleared her throat.

"Hey there," he said.

"Any chance I could borrow the pen?" she asked with a small smile.

He stilled his hand and slowly slid it across the desk to her. Her fingers brushed his as she picked it up. It was ridiculous that such a small, casual touch could make his heart pound against his ribs, but it did.

She quickly crossed a name off the reservation list and glanced up. "Is the Taylor party here yet?" she asked the room at large.

A woman raised her hand and stood with four children and a man rising at her side. Delia caught Garrett's eyes. "Be right back."

He nodded and watched her walk away, her hips swinging with her steps. Long moments later, she returned. He immediately handed the pen over. After she crossed the next name off, she returned the pen to his hand and rested her elbows on the desk. This afforded him a tantalizing view. Tiny freckles were scattered randomly. His fingertips remembered the lush give of her skin. His eyes traveled along her neck, past the soft beat of her pulse and down to the shadowed curves of her breasts. He fought the urge to lean across the desk and drag his tongue down into that valley where her skin was dewy and scented with vanilla. *Holy hell.* He was in serious trouble.

After he'd obsessed about whether or not Delia was the main reason he was so reluctant to return to Seattle, he'd reminded himself he'd never even thought of her when he walked out of that courtroom and impulsively booked his flight to Alaska. The trouble was now he couldn't sort out his feelings. She brought him to his knees, literally and figuratively. He forced his eyes back up and found hers. They held a glimmer of uncertainty, the tiny flicker making him want to wipe it out of her eyes and heart. She made him feel all kinds of things he'd never even considered—this overriding need to be with her that went beyond physical, and a desire to protect her and take care of her. He took a breath and reminded himself—*again*—where they were.

"How was your day?" he asked.

Something passed through her eyes, but it was gone before he had a chance to guess at it. She shrugged. "Okay I guess. Busy. Our hostess tonight called out sick, so I'm pulling double duty. How about you?"

"Busy. The old snowmobile got cranky today, so I spent most of the day helping Gage fix it. When all was said and done, we got it running, but that thing's on its last legs. Gage is stubborn though. He's not ready to give up on it. I'm thinking I might go behind his back and buy another new one. If I ask him about it, he'll say no."

Delia giggled and nodded. "You're absolutely right. Gage is great, but he's a fixer. My dad shares that tendency, so I'm used to it. I say go for it. He already got one new snowmobile, so he's hanging onto that old one no matter what."

Garrett nodded. "The rest of us inherited the lodge with Gage, but he's the only one working his ass off to make a go of it. I figure if all I do is help out with equipment and supplies, it'll be better than nothing."

Delia nodded and turned away when a new group of customers walked in. She checked her list and gave them a time frame before turning back to him. She picked up right where their conversation left off. "Gage doesn't mind you all aren't working up here. He says all the time that he feels lucky you guys are supporting him to try to bring the lodge back to life."

"Try? He did more than try. It's done." Garrett felt a flush of pride when he considered how hard Gage had worked to bring Last Frontier Lodge out of retirement. Before Gage moved to Alaska, he'd had a rough few years. He seemed at loose ends after he retired from active duty with the Navy SEAL's and had seemed burdened after the death of his best friend on a mission. Garrett had initially thought Gage was half-crazy to uproot himself and try to resurrect the lodge, but once he'd come up to visit over Christmas, he'd known Gage had made the right choice for him. Now, with Garrett's own misgivings about his career, he had a better sense of what Gage had been seeking—a sense of purpose that what he did mattered personally. Garrett recalled Becca's words about how she thought he'd eventually need to find something more meaningful.

Delia's voice broke into his thoughts. "You should tell him that."

"Huh?"

"That you think he's succeeded with the lodge. I think he's happy here, especially since he's met Marley, but I know he wonders here and there if you all think he's crazy. He was so happy when everyone came up for the holidays. Even though you were only here for a few days," she said with a wry grin.

Garrett nodded slowly. "Right. Maybe I will. And maybe I was only here for a few days at Christmas, but I'm here for a bit longer now. I didn't realize what I was missing."

His heart thumped—hard. He wasn't sure where he intended to go with this conversation, but for some reason, he wanted to talk with Delia about his confusion. He was saved from this impulse when Don entered the waiting area with Nick on his heels. Nick raced to Garrett's side.

"Hey Garrett! Can I help you and Gage again tomorrow?"

Garrett glanced down at Nick and ruffled his almost-black hair. "If it's okay with your mom, it's okay with me. Not sure what we'll be doing tomorrow, so you might have to wait on that."

Nick's blue eyes widened with his smile. He bounced on his heels and looked up at his mother. Delia smiled softly and shook her head. "You know I usually say yes. But," she paused, her gaze sobering. "...it depends on the weather. If it's bad out, you won't be going anywhere on the slopes."

Nick clapped his hands. "Thanks Mom!" He raced past her through the swinging door into the kitchen where he'd likely get all kinds of tasty snacks from the line cooks.

Don clapped Garrett on the shoulder and leaned against the desk beside him. "You're good with him. Not everyone's a fan of little boys who talk non-stop."

Garrett met Don's warm blue eyes. "No problem. He's a good kid."

Conversation carried on around Garrett with Delia checking in with customers and Don chatting up locals he knew. At one point, Garrett found himself alone with Don for several minutes. Don met his eyes and cleared his throat.

"Delia's my only daughter," Don offered.

Garrett held his eyes and nodded. "I know." He waited, sensing Don needed to say whatever he was about to say.

"If you're wondering, she hasn't said a word to me about you, but I've been around the block. I see the way she looks at you and vice versa." Don paused for a slow breath. "I like you and I get the feeling Delia might mean something to you. Do me a favor and just be straight with her."

Garrett stared at Don, his thoughts scrambling. Of all the situations he'd talked his way through, this one flummoxed him. Don was a good man. Garrett respected him. How the hell could he explain his feelings for Delia when he didn't fully understand them himself? Not to mention he didn't know if she reciprocated them. He realized Don was waiting. "Look, I'm not gonna lie to you. I like Delia—a lot more than I bargained on. If you're worried about my intentions, it's fair to say I don't know exactly what they are. You might think I'm out for a fling, but I'm not. When I came up here, I wasn't sure what my plans were. Right now, I'm thinking about staying for a while." He ran out of words and paused for a breath.

Don glanced through the archway into the restaurant. Delia stood by a table chatting with customers. Don turned back to Garrett. "Does Delia know you might be staying for a while?"

Garrett shrugged. "As much as I know about it. She knows I planned to be here at least a month or more. Once I know more, she'll be the first to know."

Don nodded slowly. "Got it. It's up to Delia, but be careful about what you say to Nick. He'd love to have a father. He doesn't need to get confused."

Garrett's throat tightened. "I know. I'd never do anything to confuse him."

The click of heels carried in their direction. Delia was walking their way.

Don caught his eyes briefly. "Hope you understand why I said something," he said gruffly.

Garrett nodded swiftly and turned away as Delia walked behind the desk. Her blue eyes bounced between her father and him. If she sensed anything, she elected to ignore it. "Dad, how late you plan on staying tonight? Did you need some leftovers for dinner?"

Don grinned. "Nick's probably got a full belly by now. He's been grazing in the kitchen long enough. I'll grab something and head out. You'll be working late, I suppose."

"I'll be here at least until we shut down. It's Friday, so that means a late night at the bar."

Don pushed away from the desk. "We'll leave through the back. Catch you tomorrow," he said with a wave before nudging the swinging door to the kitchen with his shoulder.

# CHAPTER 12

Garrett came awake slowly. The room was dark with only the soft light from the bathroom splashing across the bed. Delia lay beside him, her legs tangled with his. He stroked a hand down her back and curled it over her hip. He wanted nothing more than to fall back asleep with her, but he knew she wanted to get up and drive through the dark, so she could be home for Nick in the morning. He listened to the rhythmic sound of her breathing. He allowed himself a few moments of luxury, of simply laying at her side, savoring the rise and fall of her breath and her lush curves warm against his side.

He gently rocked her shoulder. "Delia," he whispered.

"Hmm?" she mumbled.

"It's one-thirty. You said you wanted to get up before two to drive home."

She lifted her head from his shoulder, her hair a rumpled mess. "It's already one-thirty?" Her voice had more strength.

"Sorry to say, but now it's…" He paused and glanced at the clock on the nightstand. The numbers glowed bright green, mocking him with their clarity. He turned back to her and brushed her hair out of her face. "...one-thirty two to be precise."

She groaned and let her head fall back to his shoulder. He chuckled and stroked her back in slow circles. "Fine with me if you want to stay, but I don't think that's what you want."

Oddly enough, there was a time when he'd have considered himself crazy to date a single mother. Too complicated, too many needs to consider. With Delia, though he desperately wanted to sleep through the night and wake in the morning with her, he didn't question the fact that she needed to go home. If it weren't for her father, who could put Nick to bed and be there for him at any point, Garrett wouldn't even blink at the fact that it would mean a rather long wait before she ever fell asleep at his side. He knew it was important to her to be there for Nick in the morning, so he'd make sure she was there. His own wants and needs took a backseat.

She lifted her head again. "Okay then. I'm getting up," she announced firmly.

When she didn't move, he chuckled. "Is this you getting up?"

"This is me working up the energy to get up."

He felt her smile in the darkness. He leaned up and caught her lips in a kiss before kicking the covers back and sitting up. "Let's do this. I'll walk you out."

Once again, he watched her drive away in the cold, dark night. There were no northern lights shimmering in the sky tonight, only a panorama of stars glittering in the inky darkness. The sound of her tires rolling across the snow-packed drive slowly faded. An owl hooted softly from the trees nearby. He took several deep breaths—the air was so cold and clean here, it was as if he could drink it in and cleanse himself inside and out.

Hours later, he sat at the kitchen table and turned on his

laptop. As promised, he was checking his work email. He could tell Elaine was pruning for him. As his assistant, she had access to his email. Without her, he'd have expected hundreds of emails, yet there were only about twenty flagged for his attention. He quickly skimmed them and replied as needed to a few. Elaine had also conveniently sent him a summary of matters of concern. To this day, he didn't know how he'd manage without her relentlessly efficient support. He clicked on his work cell and checked his messages. He'd left Carlton a message the other day just as he'd promised Elaine. Carlton had left a return message—demanding and pushy as Garrett expected.

Garrett tapped to return Carlton's call and waited.

"It's about damn time."

Carlton wasn't one for niceties, so Garrett didn't bother with them when he was dealing with Carlton.

"I already left you a message, Carlton. What else are you waiting for?"

"I will not be working with Ms. Brooks. That's unacceptable. I hired your firm to have you handle all of my cases."

Garrett took a breath. This conversation was strangely calming. Carlton represented everything he didn't like about corporate law—he was entitled, arrogant and cared little for the needs of anyone other than himself and the bottom line.

"Working with Ms. Brooks is the only option you have right now. As I'm sure Elaine explained to you, I'm currently unavailable due to a family situation and don't have a time frame for my return."

Carlton sputtered. Garrett could actually picture his face reddening.

"Well, I may have to take my business elsewhere if that's the case."

Carlton's reply was exactly what Garrett expected.

Carlton thought he was playing a poker game and was waiting for Garrett's next move. He'd yet to learn any lessons from the various legal firms that had allowed him to take his business elsewhere. He was a high maintenance client who tended to argue about everything, billing included. At one time, Garrett would have thrived on playing this imaginary game of poker. Right now, he simply didn't care about the outcome, which strengthened every move he made.

"You can do whatever you need to do, Carlton. Please notify Elaine of your decision by the end of next week. Ms. Brooks' availability will be limited after that."

He didn't wait for Carlton's reply and ended the call. His phone immediately began ringing again. He turned it off and put it back in the bottom of his duffel bag. He glanced around to find his personal phone. Spying it on the counter, he snagged it and called Elaine. She picked up immediately.

"Hello, Garrett. How are you today?"

"Just fine. Talked to Carlton a few minutes ago. He has until the end of next week to let you know what his plans are."

"What are his options?"

"Work with Olivia, or take his business elsewhere."

Elaine chuckled. "Excellent. I'll let you know when I hear from him. Did you get my email?"

"I did. Anything else I need to know?"

"Of course not. Any updates on when you'll be back?"

The sense of temporary relief he'd felt after his call with Carlton was followed with a knot of tension and uncertainty. He knew he'd have to give an answer soon, but he wasn't quite ready. He also knew his answer would involve going to Seattle and making a decision there. Whatever lay between him and Delia muddied his thoughts so much that he couldn't think clearly when he was near her.

Alaska, Diamond Creek, and the Last Frontier Lodge

also represented layer upon layer of something he was seeking. He wasn't quite sure he could see through the haze without going back to the place he once thought had been his center.

He took a deep breath and replied to Elaine. "I don't have a firm date, but it should be within the month."

*  *  *

DELIA CAREFULLY STRAIGHTENED the silverware and placemat. After they were perfectly situated, she flipped through the menu. She was restlessly waiting for Helen to arrive at the Boathouse. Her phone chirped, indicating a text had arrived. She flipped her phone over on the table. Marley was checking in.

*What time is your lunch date?*

*Now.*

*Okay then. Don't forget it's your decision. Call me when you're done.*

*Will do.*

She'd run into Marley this morning after the breakfast crowd had thinned out. Marley had given her a mini pep talk before Delia headed out to meet Nick's grandmother. Right behind Marley, Garrett had swung through her office and nudged her chin up for a kiss. When she'd mentioned Helen was coming down today, he'd nodded and asked if she needed anything. Oddly, the simple fact that he asked was enough to add fuel to the courage she was running on.

While she waited for Helen to arrive, she kept reminding herself Nick would want a chance to know his grandmother, but it didn't change the reality that meeting Helen opened a door to Terry. Though she'd lamented his absence in Nick's life, she didn't trust him. Allowing a relationship to develop with his mother provided a much closer connection to him. She fiddled with her necklace and took a breath.

An older woman approached her table. She was on the short side with long black hair streaked with silver. The same black hair Terry had passed on to Nick. Helen stopped at the side of the table, her brown eyes crinkling when she smiled hesitantly.

"Delia?"

She took a breath and smiled nervously. "Helen?"

Helen nodded. "Yes." She gestured to the chair across from Delia. "May I?"

Delia nodded. "Of course."

Helen removed her coat and hung it on her chair before taking a seat. She glanced out the windows and sighed. "Such a lovely view."

The Boathouse Café was situated on a small rise overlooking Kachemak Bay. It felt as if one was seated over the water with the building high on pilings. The glide and roll of waves lulled her. The sky was dotted with clouds today. They drifted in front of the mountains on the far side of the bay. Seagulls called and swooped along the shore.

Delia turned back to Helen. "That it is. How was your drive from Anchorage?"

"Uneventful, which means a lot in the winter in Alaska. The roads were clear and dry all the way down."

A waitress stopped by and served them water. "Should I give you ladies a few minutes?"

Helen caught Delia's eyes. "If you're ready, go ahead and order. I can take a quick look," she said as she picked up the menu.

"I'll take the halibut tacos," Delia said. "Are you sure you don't need more time?" she asked Helen.

Helen set the menu down. "No need. I'll take the salmon burger."

Their waitress jotted down their order and collected the

menus. Delia's stomach had been knotted with anxiety all morning. Now that Helen was finally here, her tension eased slightly. The anticipation was half the battle.

Helen took a sip of water. Her face was soft and kind. Her warm brown eyes held Delia's. "I'm sure this isn't easy for you. Thank you for meeting me."

"It's not, but it's important for Nick to have a chance to know you."

Somehow they plowed through the first few moments of conversation. Sometimes sticking to the superficial was incredibly helpful. The weather, the view and the latest news were safe topics. Delia recalled her mother's words so many years ago. Manners were to conversation like bread was to butter—it made things smoother. Helen was gracious and polite and had a host of questions about Last Frontier Lodge.

"Ted and I skied there a few times when we were young. How did you end up working there?"

"Believe it or not, my mother used to manage the kitchen there and my father handled the slopes and grounds. When Gage Hamilton came back to town to reopen it, he hired my father, and my father persuaded me to help with the kitchen."

"That must be wonderful! Do you enjoy it?"

"I do. I grew up cooking with my mother, so I always wanted to be a chef. Before I had Nick, I thought maybe I'd move to Seattle, but I'm glad I came back to Diamond Creek."

Their waitress arrived to serve their food. After the brief interruption, Helen shifted gears. "Your mother must be proud to see you running the same kitchen she did."

Delia experienced a flash of pain, but she'd slowly grown accustomed to her mother's absence. "My mother passed away a few years ago. Pancreatic cancer."

Helen's eyes whipped up. "I'm so sorry. I had no idea."

"That's okay. How could you have known? It wasn't easy, especially for my father, but time helps."

They ate in between snippets of conversation. After their plates had been cleared, Helen leaned back in her chair. Her gaze was somber. "I'm sure you know I'd like to meet Nick as soon as possible. I'd about given up on ever having a grandchild. I suppose we should talk about Terry. If you're worried about me trying to pressure you into involving him in Nick's life, I can assure you there's no need to worry. Terry is only intermittently in contact with me. He had a few brushes with the law after he got involved in drugs. I'd like to say I knew when that happened, but I don't. Terry and his father were close. After Ted died, things seemed to spiral out of control for Terry. I'm not making excuses for my son's complete failure to be a father to Nick. It is what it is."

Delia chewed the inside of her mouth. "I was worried about Terry. Not because I don't ever want him to have contact with Nick, but because it's not okay unless it's on my terms. Now that I've had a chance to meet you, I'm not worried you would try to force that. I suppose we should work out a time for you to meet Nick. My father would also like to meet you."

Helen clasped her hands together, her eyes glistening with tears. "Thank you, dear. Just say when and I'll make it work."

A while later, Delia walked along the beach. Helen had left with plans to return next weekend. Delia tucked her hands in her pockets and idly kicked at a pebble. A salty breeze gusted off the water. An eagle flew low across the water and landed on a piece of driftwood, regally staring out over the water. She took a breath, the biting air soothing her. The anxiety she'd been carrying ever since she'd picked up the phone and heard Terry's voice had eased. Nick would get the chance to meet his grandmother, and it felt right.

Her mind shifted gears, turning to Garrett. Thoughts of him ran in a loop in her brain these days. If only she knew what to do. The closer she got to him, the more she worried she couldn't protect her own heart. It was only a matter of time before he returned to Seattle. He'd brought her alive inside in more ways than one, but she couldn't be foolish. *But you don't know for certain what he plans to do. He's told you himself he isn't sure.* No matter how hard she tried to be rational, her silly, hopeful heart kept chiming in.

She turned back toward the parking lot. A gust of wind blew her hair wild. By the time she reached her car, she was shivering. She sat in her blessedly warm car and allowed the heat to seep through her. As she drove back up toward the lodge, she couldn't help but wonder if she'd see Garrett again tonight. The problem was she liked him far too much for her own good. Combining that with the fact she practically melted inside and out when he was anywhere near made him almost impossible for her to resist.

# CHAPTER 13

"Hey Nick, you riding up with us today?"

Garrett turned at Gage's question, recalling that Nick had asked about coming with them today. He and Gage were in the utility room off the hallway by the kitchen getting their tools organized and tugging on their winter gear. In Garrett's case, he was layering himself in borrowed winter gear from Gage. He most certainly didn't have his own. Rather, he had a closet full of almost identical suits.

Nick came skidding down the hall. "Can I?" he asked, his eyes wide with excitement.

Garrett grinned down at him. "Like I said last night, as long as it's okay with your mom. Let's go check."

He rested a hand on Nick's shoulder as they walked into the kitchen. Delia's hair was in a loose knot atop her head. A few honeyed curls had escaped and fell around her face. Her apron was streaked with a variety of colors. She was currently stirring something on the stove. Nick dashed to her side. "Mom, can I go with Garrett and Gage? You said I could if the weather was okay."

Delia paused in her stirring, her eyes snagging with his

briefly before she looked down at Nick. "I sure did." She glanced out the window. The sky was overcast with the sun breaking through here and there. "Looks good enough for now." She dropped a kiss on Nick's head and turned to Garrett. "See you when you guys get back."

Garrett kept a firm grip on the impulse to kiss her and merely nodded. Nick spun around and raced back into the hallway. Moments later, they were zooming up the slopes. They were headed to the most distant slopes today. Gage wanted to do some repair work on the roof of one of the ski huts, in addition to installing the remaining two heaters.

It was a long few hours helping Gage with the roof repair. Once they got up there, it quickly became apparent they were dealing with more than a few damaged shingles. Garrett became more impressed with Nick's behavior, and by extension Delia's parenting, because Nick was forced to wait on the ground while he and Gage climbed up and down the ladder. By the time they finished with the roof, the wind had picked up and it was freezing.

Garrett stepped into the ski hut, set the toolbox on the bench and rubbed his hands together.

"It's damn cold!"

Gage was a step behind him with Nick on his heels. He slammed the door shut and tossed his hood back. "Wind's up. Let start a fire in the woodstove while we work on the heater."

Garrett pulled his gloves off and threw them on the bench. Before he said a word, Nick opened the small wood-stove and starting placing wood inside from the rack nearby. Moments later, they had a fire going. They nibbled on snack bars from Gage's backpack before starting to work on the heater.

Roughly an hour later, Garrett slid out from behind the heater and nodded to Nick. Nick scrambled out from his position where he'd once again tightened the fittings and triumphantly tapped the on button. The very quiet hum of the heater started and warm air came out.

Nick stepped in front of Garrett, his palm held high. "High five!"

Another thwack of palms with Gage, and Nick flung himself on the bench, his eyes traveling to the window. "Uh oh. When did it start snowing?"

Garrett looked out the window to see nothing but white. Snow blew sideways, thick and heavy. "Oh..." He bit his tongue to keep from swearing. "...boy." He caught Gage's eyes. "This must've blown in fast." He stood and stared into the blinding white before plunking down on the bench.

Gage strode to the door, opening it a crack. Snow swirled inside, along with a fierce burst of wind, before Gage slammed the door shut. "I'll say. Looks like we'll be sitting tight for a bit."

Nick stood on his toes, his hands curling on the windowsill. "We can make it down okay. Let's go." He turned to them, his eyes anxious. "My mom'll get worried if I'm not back soon."

"Your mom'll give us a talking to if we take off in this weather with you," Garrett replied. "She knows it wasn't like this when we left, so you won't be in trouble for this. It's safer if we wait."

Gage nodded firmly. "Absolutely buddy. Let's give her a call and let her know." He tugged his phone out and handed it to Nick.

Nick quickly dialed and held the phone to his ear, his eyes traveling to the window over and over. "Mom? It's me. Garrett and Gage said we have to wait to come back. Is that okay?"

Garrett heard the rumble of her response while Nick nodded. "Okay. He's right here." He held the phone out to Garrett.

Delia's voice came out rapidly as soon as Garrett

brought the phone to his ear. "I tried calling you guys a little while ago when it started to snow. How come you didn't answer?" Her voice was tight, her worry reaching through the phone line and grabbing his heart.

"I'm sorry. We didn't hear the phone ring. Gage and I were working on the roof for a while. It must've started snowing not long after we came inside, but we were so busy with the heater, we didn't notice."

"Okay, okay." He heard her take a deep breath and wished he were there with her. He cursed himself and Gage for not noticing the snow coming their way.

"Can you do me a favor and stay put until this blows over?" she asked.

"That's why we called. We're sitting tight until the visibility is better. We'll stay until you're comfortable with us heading down. Okay?"

"Okay. Please tell me you got the heater running."

Garrett could see her wry smile, could sense her trying to tamp down her worry. "Yup. It's running. Nick's a pro at these now. We also have the woodstove and plenty of wood stacked in the corner."

Her laugh had a forced edge to it. He wished like hell he didn't have the audience of his way too perceptive brother and Delia's curious son in the small hut. He wanted to say something to soothe her, but privacy was impossible. "Okay if we check in in a little bit? We should have an idea if this snow is going to slow down sometime soon."

"That would be great. Can you put Nick back on?"

"Of course. Here he is."

He handed the phone to Nick. He leaned his head against the wall while Nick chattered with his mother, excitedly giving her a summary of their day. Gage caught his eyes and arched a brow. He slid across the bench, which stretched across the entire wall, and came to a stop beside Garrett.

"News flash. You can stop trying to play it low with Delia. The way you feel about her is all over your face," Gage said, his voice just above a whisper.

Garrett's heart thumped—hard—in his chest. Gage pushed away a little. Garrett looked up and met Gage's knowing eyes. "That obvious, huh?"

Gage shrugged. "Another time, maybe not. Since I recognize that look now, yeah."

Nick was still busy talking to Delia. Garrett ran a hand through his hair. "You recognize it?"

Gage held his eyes, his gaze steady with a hint of concern. "I saw it every time I looked in that mirror after I met Marley."

Garrett's chest tightened with emotion. He wasn't ready to put words to how he felt about Delia. Gage loved Marley, really loved her. It scared the hell out of Garrett to consider *love* might be what he felt for Delia.

* * *

DELIA THREW HERSELF INTO BAKING. Kneading dough and prepping pastries could keep her busy for hours. She needed busy right now. Rationally, she knew it was just a snowstorm. She'd been born and raised in Alaska and been through more snowstorms than she could count. Yet, she didn't feel comfortable with Nick high up on the mountain in a tiny ski hut. Even with Garrett and Gage there and the knowledge he was warm and snug inside, anxiety bloomed in her chest.

As the hours passed, the wind increased in its intensity, howling outside, the snow flying so hard and fast it pelted against the windows. Skiers had been streaming in from the slopes for the last few hours. As usual, there were a few stragglers. The kitchen staff pumped food out and the bar kept drinks flowing as darkness fell.

Delia slid another tray of pastries in the oven when her father came into the kitchen and leaned against the baking table. "What's up, Dad?"

Don's eyes were sober. "Two missing skiers. Our best bet is to ask Gage and Garrett to check on them. They were up on the advanced slopes."

The anxiety she'd been managing to hold at bay flashed through her. Only an hour ago, Nick had called to check in and reported they were playing cards and eating snacks.

"Are you sure that's the best option?"

Don nodded slowly. "Any of us down here will be fighting to get up there in this wind. It's two teenage boys. Their parents are pretty stressed out. I wished they'd reported it sooner, but they said they kept thinking the boys would make it back."

Delia knew what he suggested was the most sensible plan, but she didn't want Garrett to leave the ski hut. She knew they would tell Nick to stay put. Her worry ballooned, but she fought to keep it from showing.

"I guess that's what we do then. Have you called up there yet?"

Don shook his head. "Wanted you to know before I did. I'll call right now."

Don stepped away, tucking his phone against his shoulder. The murmur of his voice carried to her. She needed to be alone and walked to her office, shutting the door behind her. Moments later, there was a quick knock and her father stepped inside.

"Gage said they'd head out in a few minutes. He promised me Nick wouldn't be leaving the ski hut. I talked to Nick as well. He knows outside is no place for him right now, so don't worry about him."

She knew Nick would know everyone wanted him to stay put, but that didn't mean he wouldn't make a poor choice at the wrong time. She batted that worry away and nodded quickly, her throat tight with emotion.

Her father cleared his throat. "Garrett can take care of himself. He'll be okay."

Her head whipped up. "Dad…"

"Honey, I know you've been trying to be discreet, but I see the way you look at him. No need to hide from me, you know. I worry about you, but you get to make your own decisions."

Tears were hot against the back of her eyelids. She took a shuddering breath. "I wasn't trying to hide anything. I just…ugh. I don't know, Dad. I can't talk about this right now. I just need to know they're gonna be okay. Maybe Garrett can take care of himself, but he hasn't had much experience with snow like this. He only just learned how to drive the damn snowmobile since he got here a few weeks ago. This weather is no joke!"

Her father slipped his arm across her shoulders and gave her a squeeze. "I know, hon. He might be new to this weather and just getting the hang of driving in it, but he's quick and has good judgment. Gage'll be with him too."

She rubbed her eyes and gulped in air. "I know, I know."

Her father gave her another squeeze and stepped away. "Gage said he'd call in as soon as they have an update. Nick has his phone, and they have Garrett's. They also have radio back up. Now get out there and get to work. I know you, if you don't do something, you'll pace a groove in the floor."

Delia shook her head and went back into the kitchen to get to work. Another hour later, her father pushed through the swinging door again.

"Gage found the boys."

She knew from the look on her father's face that there was more. "And?"

"Garrett hasn't made it back yet."

# CHAPTER 14

Garrett squinted against the blowing snow. He and
Gage had headed out after mapping out where
they'd crisscross the slopes to try to find the
missing skiers. He could see the light from Gage's snowmobile in the distance through the trees between the two
slopes. He paused to turn along the edge of the slope. He
heard the high-pitched whine of the engine and felt the
snowmobile catch and then tilt sideways. He tumbled down
the outer edge of the ski slope, grunting when he came to a
hard stop against what could only be a boulder. Snow stung
his face, blowing sideways in vicious gusts. Visibility was all
but non-existent. He shifted his position and tried to see
how far he'd fallen. There was nothing to see other than the
blur of snow and darkness. Above him, he could see the
light from the snowmobile pointing into the sky, needlessly
lighting the way up.

\* \* \*

"Come here," Marley said, looping her arm around Delia's

and practically dragging her to a booth in the corner of the restaurant. Ginger came through the entrance from the front and dashed over to the booth, skidding into the seat.

"Made it!" she declared. When she caught a look at Delia's face, Ginger turned immediately to Marley. "Where's the alcohol?"

"Coming right up," Marley replied. She loosened her hold on Delia's arm. "Sit down. You're driving yourself crazy not getting a damn bit of actual work done. Be right back."

Delia sat down with a sigh as Marley headed over to the bar. The snowstorm still raged outside and the restaurant was fuller than usual at this hour, although the tone was quiet. The nearest cell and radio tower had been knocked out roughly an hour ago, so there was no news on the status up on the mountain. Delia knew Marley had a point. She'd been trying to keep herself busy with work. After she ruined a batch of potato leek soup and forgot to add yeast to a batch of dough, which she only discovered after kneading it pointlessly for too long, she'd taken to pacing back and forth in the kitchen.

Harry, her steady front-staff supervisor, paused by their booth. "Don't blame Marley for dragging you out. I sent her your way. You need to try something else to calm down. I figured friends might be more helpful than trying to wear the finish off the floor."

Delia looked up at him and fought the tears threatening. Harry slipped his arm across her shoulders and gave her a squeeze. "Hang in there. I'm around if you need anything." At that, he moved on, filling waters and coffees as he wove through the tables.

Marley returned with two bottles of wine and three glasses. After Delia took several gulps, she set her wineglass down and sighed. "This sucks."

Ginger nodded emphatically. "Hell yeah, it sucks! You're

stuck here waiting while Nick is sitting in a teeny tiny ski hut at the top of the damn mountain. And then there's your boyfriend. By the way, I won't give you any shit tonight for not bothering to give me an update on Garrett." Her eyes softened and she reached across the table to grip Delia's hand. "They'll be okay. We have to think that."

Marley caught her eyes. "Gage will find Garrett. Right before we lost reception, he told me they could see the light from Garrett's snowmobile. I'm not going to pretend it'll be a breeze in this weather, but Gage will find him and get him safe." Marley appeared to be fighting back her own tears.

Delia realized she wasn't the only one who had loved ones to worry about. Gage was probably out right now in the biting winter wind and blinding snow trying to find Garrett. He'd already tracked down the two teen boys. The last word they had was Gage had been headed to the ski hut with the boys before planning to turn back to find Garrett.

Delia took another gulp of wine and glanced around the restaurant. A couple at one of the tables by the windows was huddled together. "That must be…"

"The boys' parents," Marley finished for her. "Even though we heard from Gage that he located them, we lost reception before he confirmed they made it back to the ski hut."

Delia's stomach churned. She felt for them—a deep, visceral understanding of their worry. At least she knew her own son was warm and safe in the hut. A very small voice, which she batted back every time it tried to make itself heard, worried Nick might have tried to go out and help on his own. She must have reminded herself five thousand times that Nick had been warned time and again about the dangers of going outside during a snowstorm like this. She just prayed and prayed that he wouldn't try to get overly helpful with Gage and Garrett out in the storm.

Her brain was running on two tracks. One moment, she

spun through worries about Nick. The next, fear raced through her for Garrett. She could hardly stand to think about where he was with the wind battering in gusts against the windows. The lodge had lost power over an hour ago and was running on generators. Snow flew in icy pellets, the sound like sharp rain on the windows. Snow and wind like this stung the skin. With the cold, it would burn. Aside from the small ski huts up on the mountain, there was no shelter for Garrett, so he would be freezing. Even the best winter gear could only help so much in weather like this.

# CHAPTER 15

*G*arrett tightened his hood and tucked his hands into his pockets. As he settled into the spot he'd fallen, the force of his fall started to seep into his bones. His shoulder ached and his knee throbbed. His hopes of a quick rescue started to wane by the time he was shivering forcefully. Thoughts of Delia filled his mind. Not much was clear for him lately, but what he felt for her took his breath away. The word love feathered its way into his thoughts. His chest ached and not solely because he fell. He didn't know how much time passed when he heard someone calling his name. He must have drifted in and out of a sleepy state. He slowly came to and started to stand before he remembered where he was.

"Down here!" he called.

He heard motion through the snow and then Gage's voice from above. "Got you! Give me a sec. I'm gonna get a light shining down there, so we can see enough to get you up."

Garrett waited in the cold, shivers wracking his body. He heard another voice with Gage, but he didn't recognize it. Eventually, a light beamed down upon him and Gage climbed down beside him. It was too windy for conversation to be anything other than shouts over the wind, so Gage worked in silence. He hooked a belt around Garrett's waist and helped him clamber up the steep incline. Long moments later, Garrett was sitting behind Gage on the snowmobile. Gage must have found the missing teens. One of them was with him and had turned Garrett's snowmobile upright. With Gage leading the way, the young man followed them through the snowy dark, wind whipping at them, until they reached the ski hut. The tiny square of light shining through the window brought a wash of relief coursing through Garrett.

* * *

TIME PASSED SLOWLY. Marley and Ginger were steady, reliable, dear friends. They alternated with soothing support and distraction. The wine helped. It softened the edges of her worry and dulled the frantic feeling that spun inside. Her father stopped by the table occasionally, but he was busy monitoring the generators and doing just about anything that needed to be done.

Delia lost all track of time when the radio Marley had sitting on the table crackled. Don came striding to the table a second later. "Got it. One of the kids here spent the last three hours fiddling with the signals. No idea how he pulled it off, but he got the radios to work on another frequency. The downed tower isn't a problem, but the connection's shitty."

Delia fumbled for the radio and dropped it immediately. Don held up the one in his hand. "I'll try."

Delia's heart felt like it was going to pound out of her chest. Ginger scooted closer to her on the bench and gave her a quick hug. "Breathe." After Delia gulped in some air,

Ginger refilled her wineglass. "And have a sip of wine. It helps."

After several minutes of static and more than a few swallows of wine, Nick's voice crackled over the radio. "Granddad?"

Don grinned widely. "That's right, buddy. Glad you stayed put like you were supposed to. How's it going up there?"

Between fits and starts, Nick managed to update them he was warm and toasty, along with Gage, the two teens and Garrett. Tears were hot in Delia's eyes as she listened to Nick cheerfully summarize everything. He sounded slightly frightened at a few points, but his joy and relief at Gage and Garrett's safe return was palpable through the crackly radio.

Gage got on and checked in about a few logistics. "It looks like we're in for the night. Garrett finally fell asleep a few minutes ago, but he's pretty banged up. Even if the snow stops, I don't want to try to move him in the dark."

Delia's chest tightened and she fought the tide of worry rising inside. Garrett was safe. She just had to wait through the night until she could see him. Ginger gave her another squeeze. The radio fuzzed. Through the broken connection, she heard Gage quickly tell Marley he loved her.

Hours later as she woke from her fitful sleep, she couldn't help but wish maybe, just maybe, she and Garrett could have something like what Gage and Marley had. If only she knew what Garrett felt. As her mind ran along its familiar tracks, she considered perhaps she might need to dredge up the courage to tell Garrett how she felt even if she didn't know how he felt in return. The mere thought sent her heart pounding. Restless, she rolled over on the couch in Marley and Gage's living room and glanced out the windows. Light was just barely starting to filter through. The wind had stopped and snow was falling gently. Last night's storm had blown in and out, and it was as if it had never happened.

* * *

GARRETT WOKE, his body aching from head to toe. He turned his head very slowly and glanced around the room. He was on the floor in the small building, along with Gage, Nick and the two teen boys they'd been looking for last night. He vaguely remembered getting back here, but he had no recollection of anything other than how good it felt to be warm again.

Nick rolled over and lifted his head. "Garrett!" He scrambled up and grinned.

Garrett started to sit up and pain shot through his shoulder. Every inch of him ached. Nick's expression shifted to worried. "Are you okay?" He climbed across the two boys and stepped on Gage's foot on his way to Garrett's side.

"Mornin' Nick. Don't worry about me," Gage said wryly.

Nick knelt by Garrett and helped him sit up. Gage sat up and eyed Garrett. "Not looking your best this morning, but you'll do."

Garrett chuckled, discovering that even laughing hurt. "Whatever. Just glad to be here. I'm remembering why I thought law was a good career choice."

"Why's that?" Gage asked.

"Because I don't have to worry about falling down the side of a damn mountain in a snowstorm."

Gage grinned and turned away. A while later, Garrett was waiting on the snowmobile. He'd been introduced— again—to Danny and Eric. They were gregarious, helpful, and slightly cowed from their brush with danger last night. One of them was to ski down while the other drove Garrett's snowmobile down the mountain with Nick on the back.

On the ride down, Garrett felt every single bump even though Gage maneuvered slowly. Eric beat them down the hill on his skis and was waiting when they got there, surrounded by his parents and a cluster of others. The only person Garrett saw was Delia. He moved much slower than he wanted, but managed to make his way to the stairs. Delia hugged Nick close before standing and walked to meet Garrett.

His heart felt so full, he could hardly breathe. It didn't even cross his mind that they had an audience. The throbbing ache in every corner of his body forgotten, he stepped to her, cupped her cheeks and brought his lips to hers, capturing them in a lingering kiss before wrapping her in his arms and holding tight.

# CHAPTER 16

Delia walked upstairs slowly. It had been another busy day in the kitchen. Gage had bundled Garrett off for a quick trip to the doctor after they got back this morning. At loose ends, she'd gone home and managed to get Nick settled down. Her father had shooed her out not much later.

"You're damn near driving me crazy. You're too restless. Go to work and check on Garrett."

When she was walking out, he called her name.

"What?"

"Don't expect you home tonight," he said with a grin.

She shook her head, chuckling to herself as she recalled her father's comment. She made it to the top of the stairs and turned down the hall where Garrett's suite was. He'd texted to tell her he was rested and wanted to see her as soon as she could get up there.

At her knock, the door opened seconds later. Garrett stood there, his dark hair slightly rumpled and his navy eyes on her. He wore sweatpants and a worn t-shirt, his muscles accentuated under the soft fabric. Her pulse took a leap and wet heat coiled inside. Garrett didn't say a word, merely reached for her and pulled her inside, right into his strong embrace.

His eyes seared into her as his mouth descended, catching hers in a scorching kiss. In a flash, heat twisted through her. His tongue swept inside, stroking against hers, as his hands explored her curves. She flexed and arched into his touch. It was imperceptible, but she felt him flinch. She tore her lips away from his.

"You need to take it easy!" She took a step back, bumping against the door.

He shook his head. "I'm fine."

He put a hand on the door and stroked the other down the side of her neck. Toying with a lock of her hair, his eyes nearly burned her up. Every little touch sent shivers through her. She fought to keep her body under control and put a hand on his chest, softly nudging him away.

"I'm sure you are, but let's take it slow. You took a hell of a tumble last night and almost froze to death."

She shimmied away from the door and strode to the kitchen area. "Did you have something to eat yet?"

He shrugged. His stomach growled, answering for him. His smile turned sheepish. "Maybe not."

"I'll be right back." She whirled away, flinging the door open and racing back downstairs to the kitchen. She returned to his room carrying a tray filled with food from the evening's buffet selection.

They had an impromptu dinner on his bed. A while later, it occurred to Delia that she hadn't laughed so much in years. Garrett carefully carried the tray to the kitchen counter and turned to face her. His eyes darkened and sent her pulse wild with nothing more than a look. He walked deliberately toward the bed. She was seated on the edge, her bare feet dangling off the side.

He leaned down, his palms coming to either side of her hips.

"You're not stopping me now."

His gruff words ruffled across her skin, sending hot slivers of heat through her. When he kissed her this time, she tumbled into the cauldron that simmered under the surface of every moment with him. The mattress gave under the weight of his knee when he slid it between her thighs, barely nudging it against the center of her desire. She moaned into his mouth, arching into his touch.

Moment after moment passed in the blur of sensation ebbing and flowing through her. Clothes were torn off and tossed on the floor. They rolled on the bed, touching, licking and tasting. Delia pulled back long enough to see Garrett's shoulder was bruised badly. He bore several bruises on his chest and back, contusions from his collision with a few boulders. As she rolled over and sat astride him, she paused and carefully caressed his shoulder. Her throat tightened with emotion. The depth of her desire mingled with an intimacy that reached deep inside.

She cupped his cheek, his stubble rough against her palm. "I was scared last night." Her voice fractured on a sob.

His hand stroked up her abdomen, between her breasts, and threaded into her hair. "I'm okay. You were all I could think of last night." He swallowed and took a gulp of air before tugging her down for a kiss.

His kisses were masterful—searing, wet, and sense stealing. The heat flashed into fire. She curled her legs against his sides and teased him. His cock was hot and hard under the slide of her folds. She slid down his body and took him in her mouth. She thrilled to his groan and set to drive him as wild as he drove her—licking, sucking and stroking. Only when her name fell hoarsely from his lips did she drag her mouth away and straddle him again.

She was so desperate to feel him inside of her she didn't

hear him when he tried to stop her. She rose up, positioned her hips and arched down onto him, bringing him fully inside, her head falling back at the feel of him stretching her, slightly easing her desperate chase for pleasure. When she opened her eyes, his were on her with a grimace.

"What?" she asked.

"You didn't give me a chance to get a condom on."

* * *

GARRETT GESTURED TO THE NIGHTSTAND, which appeared to be miles away at the moment. All he could think was that he'd never felt anything as good as the creamy clench of her channel around his cock. His chest tightened—an unfamiliar beat of intimacy wove between them. It took all of his discipline to remain still when all he wanted to do was lift his hips and arch deeper into her.

"I'm on the pill and have been for years." She shrugged with a sheepish smile. "Kind of a habit after I had Nick. I never miss a day, so you don't need to worry. Not to mention it's been six years since I've been with anyone else."

He had to fight to think clearly. He was practically religious about using condoms, but he trusted Delia completely. And *holy hell* did she feel good around him. Slick, wet, and warm—merely holding still inside of her was the hottest experience he'd ever had. "If it's okay with you, it's more than fine with me."

Delia's blue eyes locked on his as she began to roll her hips. She started slow and picked up speed. He gripped her hips with his hands, the soft flesh giving under his touch. The push and pull of her channel pulsing around him drove him higher and higher. He held on and stroked his thumb against her clit. Her channel convulsed around him and her head fell back on a cry. He drove his hips deeper into her, his own release crashing through him.

When her head fell forward, he stroked his palm up her back, slowly bringing her into his embrace. As she rested against him, her skin damp with the sheen of passion, his heart gave, opening to something he'd never expected. This woman—so sexy, so warm, so kind and so damn unexpected—had slayed him in more ways than one.

# CHAPTER 17

*D*elia woke, warm in Garrett's arms. She smiled against his shoulder. She'd finally gotten her wish—to wake up beside him. The wispy light of morning filtered through the windows. She slowly pushed up on her elbow, careful not to disturb him, and looked outside. The sky was hazy. The sun had yet to rise from behind the mountains across the bay, but it was being shepherded in with streamers of lavender and pink shot through with soft rays of gold.

She looked down at Garrett. The sheet had fallen away from his chest. The bruising had set in around his shoulder in deep shades of purple and blue. Her stomach tightened. She forced herself to look away. She couldn't doubt the depth of her feelings for him, but she didn't think it was wise to let her too-hopeful heart forget the need to be cautious. She recalled her consideration of telling him how she felt and wasn't quite sure she had the nerve yet. This— whatever it was—between them wasn't part of his real life. Even if he considered her much more than a fling, it didn't change the reality of their circumstances. He was a high profile, corporate lawyer in Seattle. She was a single mother whose life was tethered to Diamond Creek, Alaska—a far cry from the life Garrett led in Seattle.

She took a breath and slowly sat up. Garrett rolled his head to the side. "Morning," he said, his voice gravelly with sleep.

She pushed her worries away and allowed herself this moment. Dipping forward, her hair fell around his face as she kissed him—a sleepy, soft kiss, the kind of kiss that only happened in the morning.

When she pulled away, need was pulsing through her. That's how bad it was. She'd had not one, not two, but three earth-shattering orgasms last night, and still this morning a simple kiss could send heat spiraling through her.

Garrett tried to sit up and flinched. "Damn. I keep forgetting I got hurt."

She sat back on her heels. "You're resting today," she ordered. "I'm going to go down and bring some breakfast up for you." She scrambled off the bed and walked over to his side. She carefully adjusted the pillows behind him and helped him sit up.

He protested, but she knew how tired he was given that he argued the point weakly. She left him with the television remote in hand and returned shortly thereafter with a breakfast tray. When she pushed through the door, Garrett was on the phone.

"Carlton, that's the deal. Ms. Brooks can handle your cases."

Garrett waved for her to enter the room, so she did. He was nodding to whatever was being said on the other end of the phone.

"That decision is final. Even if I return, Ms. Brooks will be handling your cases."

Delia's heart soared at the word 'if' from Garrett. *Maybe that means he's thinking about staying longer.* Hope tap-danced for a moment before she got a grip. She busied herself need-lessly straightening items on the tray.

Garrett ended the call and tossed his phone on the bed. "Let me tell you, if you want to meet a few assholes, try being a corporate lawyer."

"Oh?" She kept her voice carefully bland.

He caught her eyes, his expression shifting from annoyed to uncertain. "Look... I suppose we should talk..."

Her heart galloped away, emotion spinning through her. She stammered a few words out. "I, um, maybe... Ugh." She dropped her face in her hands and took a shuddering breath. She was acting like an idiot. Her thoughts ran wild for a moment. She considered telling him the truth she knew—she thought she was falling in love with him. She was almost ready, but she didn't want to ruin the first time she'd gotten the chance to wake up with him.

"We probably should, but can we give it a rain check this morning?" she finally asked.

Garrett's eyes held hers for a long moment as she stood at the foot of the bed. When he didn't say anything, she continued, the words falling out of her mouth, too many steps ahead of her brain. "I just wanted to enjoy the morning with you. It's the first time we got to wake up together." As soon as she heard what she said, her face heated. If Garrett didn't already think she was foolish, he would now.

A slow smile spread across his face, easing the anxiety blooming inside of her. "Sounds perfect."

Fluttery joy spread through her. She grinned and turned to pick up the breakfast tray.

* * *

GARRETT SPENT most of his day catching up on work email. After Delia left him to his own devices on the heels of a stern lecture about resting, he decided to face the work he'd been putting off. He called Elaine to ask her to set loose the gates on his email and spent hours trying to get caught up. Elaine sent over some filings Olivia had prepared on some of his hot cases. He enjoyed reviewing her work and spent hours back and forth with her over email on strategy and preparation for a few cases. Around midday, Gage showed up and handed him a bowl of stew from the kitchen.

Garrett joined Gage at the small table. "Damn, this is good," he said after a few bites of the rich, hearty potato leek stew.

"Thought you might like it. Delia made it. Basically everything she makes is delicious." Gage stood and grabbed two bottles of water from the small refrigerator before returning to the table. "How ya feelin' today?"

Garrett carefully rolled his shoulder, testing it. "Sore, but okay. Could definitely be worse." He took another few bites of stew and sat back. "Thanks for tracking me down in that storm. It was damn cold. Still not sure how I fell."

"As if there was any question I'd track you down." Gage shook his head, his eyes somber. "I knew you couldn't be far. The lights from your snowmobile were pretty helpful," he offered with a chuckle. "My guess is the track got caught on the edge of a boulder and turned you sideways too fast to stay upright. Happens all the time. Usually wouldn't be a big deal, but the weather was hell. Gave you a good taste of winter in Alaska though."

Garrett chuckled. "Guess so."

Gage eyed him, his gaze assessing. "You plan to talk about what's up with you and Delia anytime soon?"

Garrett shifted uncomfortably in his chair and delayed his answer with a few more bites. The savory stew was starting to fill him up. He hadn't noticed how hungry he'd gotten while he was working. He was considered an anomaly in the world of lawyers in that he could happily immerse himself in preparing and reviewing legal filings. The mental thinking required for those laid the ground-work for him in all of his cases. Though he loved the thrill of arguing a case in court, it was his hours of research and preparation that poised him to win case after case in court.

Gage cleared his throat. Garrett brought his attention back to Gage. "It's not that I'm trying to avoid talking about Delia, it's that I don't know what the hell to say."

Gage nodded slowly. "Have you tried talking to Delia?"

"Actually, I told her this morning we should talk and she put me off."

"I bet you didn't mind that a bit."

Garrett shrugged. "Maybe not, but I tried." He paused and took a breath, considering what to say. What passed through his mind was the way Delia looked last night when she was above him—her eyes dark with passion, her body soft and lush, her channel slick around his cock. Then, the way she felt curled against him, her skin warm against his as she relaxed into his embrace. And then, the way he felt inside through it all—as if his heart was going to fly out of his chest, an intimacy unlike anything he'd ever experienced.

He turned to look out the window at the breathtaking view that was here everyday. The evergreens marched up the mountain, giving way only for the groomed ski slopes. In the distance, Kachemak Bay glittered bright under the sun. A raven called as it flew past the windows and landed on the deck railing below. The view was simultaneously energizing and soothing.

He swung his gaze back to Gage. "Hell, I don't know what to do. I wasn't thinking straight when I hopped on a plane and flew up here, but I sure as hell wasn't thinking about Delia. Now, I can't stop thinking about her and I'm all mixed up. I don't know what to do about work, and I can hardly stand to think about being away from her." He groaned and ran a hand through his hair. "Any suggestions?"

Gage leaned back in his chair, quiet for a long moment. "For your work, you've already heard what I think. I don't know what that means as to where you live and work, but it is what it is. You and Delia? That's something else altogether. Maybe I'm biased because I had my own wake up call with Marley, but it's plain as day Delia means a lot to you. Don't let her pass you by just because you didn't plan on it. Or because it scares you."

Garrett's chest got tight. He didn't know what the hell he meant to do about Delia, but he couldn't conceive of simply saying goodbye and going back to his life without her being a part of it. He knew she felt something for him. Even though he was swimming in uncharted waters here, he was willing to bet her feelings ran deep. All his years of slick experience with women were an utter waste to him now. He was the master at flirting and keeping things casual and superficial. He was useless at navigating the uncharted emotional ground between him and Delia.

He caught Gage's eyes on him, his expression one of wry sympathy. Gage shrugged. "Been right where you are. You'll figure it out. It might help to talk to Delia."

Gage stood and headed for the door. "Meet me later for a few beers?"

At Garrett's nod, Gage left. Garrett finished his bowl of stew, savoring every bite more than usual because he knew Delia made it. He brought his laptop over to the table and kept working.

By late afternoon, he was restless and his mind was spinning with thoughts of Delia and what the hell to do. He wasn't ready to throw the towel in on his law practice. His forays back into legal strategizing today reminded him what he loved about his work and that he was damn good at it. His challenge was how to find a way to channel that into something more rewarding than working for assholes like Carlton.

Every other thought revolved around Delia. Finally, he shut his laptop and called Becca.

"Hey sis, how's it going in Seattle?"

"It's raining, and I'm headed into a late night at work getting ready for a trial tomorrow. What's up with you?"

"I don't know what the hell to do, so I figured I'd better call you. For once, I'd like someone to tell me what to do."

Becca laughed long and hard, bringing a smile to Garrett's face. "I know, I know. You've been waiting for this day since we were born."

Her laughter wound down, and he could imagine her face sobering, concern replacing her amusement. "Tell me what's going on."

Garrett started talking. In the course of doing so, one thing became clear. He knew what he needed to do about work. He needed to stop focusing solely on corporate work and do precisely as Becca had suggested already and find cases that mattered more. He had several attorneys on staff who'd be happy to take on most of the corporate work. The issue that sent him stumbling onto a plane to Alaska illuminated into clarity. His feelings for Delia were another matter altogether.

"You want me to tell you what to do? I got that when it comes to your job, and it sounds like you've figured it out yourself. It's not too complicated. I can send non-profit cases your way all day long. You should also consider consulting on some criminal cases too. You're kickass in court. So, we solved that. Onto Delia."

"I was getting to her next."

"Gage thinks you're in love with her."

"I..."

"He also thinks she's in love with you."

Garrett heart stuttered and then galloped forward. He

turned the word over in his mind. *Love.* Love was something he'd never planned to consider. Relationships were messy. He was lucky enough to have parents who loved each other and a boisterous, loving family. But he'd channeled all of his energy into work. He enjoyed women, but he hadn't encountered any woman who interested him beyond superficial and flirty levels. Until Delia. She brought him to his knees, threw him off center, and made him realize just how little he knew about love.

"That's what Gage thinks, huh?"

"Yeah. What do you think?"

Garrett stood and walked to the windows, restless and churning with emotion.

"I don't know what I think. It's... Ah hell, Becca. Delia came out of nowhere for me. I don't have much experience with..."

"Feelings," Becca offered helpfully.

At his long pause, she continued. "I'm sorry, Garrett. I didn't mean for it to sound like that. You have plenty of experience with feelings. You're an awesome brother and a great friend. You just never left any room for women to be much more than superficial in your life. You never asked for my opinion, but I'll give it to you now. I think you did that for two reasons. You're a workaholic, and I think you knew if you let yourself fall for someone, you'd fall hard. Because you're that kind of guy—you don't do anything in half measures."

"No, I guess not." He stared outside. He looked up beyond the ski slopes at the mountains stretching across the horizon. The sun was slipping slowly down the sky, glowing reddish-orange and streaking the sky with its faded rays. He ran a hand through his hair.

"Maybe you should talk to Delia," Becca offered softly.

"Gage said the same thing."

Becca chuckled. "Once in a while, Gage and I agree."

Garrett smiled and turned away from the window. "Maybe I need to get back to Seattle and make some sense of my life."

"You'd better talk to her first. You might blow it if you don't."

"I will."

He heard someone's voice in the background through his phone. Becca's voice was muted and then she came back on. "Duty calls. I can call you later tonight if you want."

"No worries. Thanks for listening. Good luck with your trial tomorrow."

"Anytime. Call me if you need to talk again."

# CHAPTER 18

"Mom!" Nick ran down the hallway toward the front door, skidding in his socked feet as he reached her.

"Hey there, how was school today?"

She dropped a quick kiss on the top of his head and started to move past him. Nick stood still and looked up at her, his blue eyes questioning. "You forgot about today."

Delia's mind whirred as she tried to think of what Nick meant. "Oh no! I'm sorry, Nick. I can't believe I forgot." Delia froze in the hallway. Helen would be here to meet Nick this afternoon. She'd been so busy at work, it had completely slipped her mind. She took a breath and glanced at her watch.

"It's okay. She won't be here for another half hour."

Nick nodded. His eyes were a mix of excitement and worry. When she told him about his grandmother, he'd spun like a top. His excitement over meeting her was tempered by the disappointment that meeting his father was still a distant, unrealized hope in his mind. She didn't quite know how to manage that, other than to be matter of fact about the situation. Honesty was messy and painful sometimes, but she couldn't think of a better option.

An hour later, Delia leaned against the kitchen counter and watched Nick chattering away with Helen. Her father was with them at the table, his easy-going manner had smoothed the way at the beginning of their meeting. Helen's expression was one of soft joy. The ball of anxiety Delia had been carrying inside eased. There were no instructions for how to navigate this emotionally loaded territory. For the thousandth time and then some, she shoved away her worn anger toward Terry. His complete lack of involvement in Nick's life added layers of complication to any potential relationship on his side of the family. Having already loved and lost one grandmother, the gift of getting to know another mattered—a lot.

After dinner, Helen helped clear the table and clean up. She came to Delia's side in the kitchen. "Thank you," she said softly.

Delia wiped her hands on a towel and turned to Helen. "I could say the same to you." She looked through the kitchen to the small den on the opposite side of the counter. Nick was in the thick of playing his allotted half hour of video games. He would be exhausted within the hour and probably fall asleep on the couch. Helen left with promises to stay in touch after Nick did, in fact, fall asleep on the couch.

Delia pulled her hair loose from its braid and stared at herself in the bathroom mirror. She tried to see what Garrett might. Her blonde hair was rumpled, as it almost always was. Her eyes looked weary. A long day at work tended to do that. She ran a brush through her hair and turned away, tugging on her softest pair of sweats and an old t-shirt. She idly flipped through the channels as she rested in bed. Garrett's absence was a sharp ache. All she'd had was one night with him and now she felt bereft without him. This, even though she was the one who insisted she couldn't see him tonight. He was starting to mean too much, her heart was too hopeful. The reality was he would most likely return to Seattle soon, and she'd need to readjust to life in Diamond Creek without him.

She fell asleep with a comedy show murmuring in the background. When she woke during the night and got up to turn off the lights, her phone blinked with a text. Tugging the covers over her again, she grabbed her phone to check.

*Missed you tonight. Good night.*

Her heart thumped with a beat of joy. Though the rational part of her mind argued against it, she texted him back anyway. Because even if it didn't last, she was going to enjoy this.

*Missed you too. Sleep tight.*

As soon as she set her phone down, it chirped again.

*I'd be sleeping much better if you were here.*

She giggled, joy racing through her. Hope danced on its toes, twirling madly. She bit her lip as she considered whether to reply.

*Would you really be sleeping?*

She giggled when she hit send, her eyes on the screen waiting for his reply.

*Probably not. In fact, I could think of all kinds of other things to do...*

She flushed, straight through, and sighed.

*Not much we can do about that now.*

*Nope. How did tonight go?*

Delia's heart flipped slowly. Leave it to Garrett to tighten his grip on her heart and body by being considerate and asking about tonight. He'd known how anxious she'd been to have Nick meet his grandmother finally.

* * *

GARRETT SPENT the morning helping Gage install the last

heater. He stood outside the small ski hut while Gage finished loading up the tools. Today was cold and clear, the sun glittering in the bright blue sky. He took a deep breath, savoring the bite of icy air. He slowly spun in a circle, taking in the breathtaking view. Atop the mountain, he had a panoramic view. The surface of the bay ruffled in the wind. Boats moved in and out of the harbor. Mount Augustine, one of the nearby volcanoes, stood tall and still in the distance. Its peak was arrayed with its own clouds. In another direction, the mountains stretched as far as he could see. An eagle screeched and lifted from the trees, its wings casting a wide shadow on the snow as it flew across the ski slope.

He circled back to look down the ski slope. Last Frontier Lodge sat at the bottom, a charming cluster of buildings. After spending more time here, he had a better under-standing of what drove Gage to return to Diamond Creek. The sound of the door closing brought his attention full circle. Gage stepped out with a duffel bag slung over his shoulder and his bag of tools in hand.

"Ready?" Gage asked.

"Let's go."

Garrett savored the cold wind on his face as they zipped down the mountain. They headed inside for a late lunch. Delia was busy in the kitchen, but she threw him a smile from across the room. He kept a tight rein on his impulses —because what he wanted to do was drag her upstairs and spend hours tangled up with her.

Awhile later, he was deep in the middle of working on some legal briefs when his phone rang. He'd notified Elaine she could call if needed while he was online. Her number flashed on his phone.

"Hey Elaine," he said, tucking his phone against his shoulder while he kept typing away.

"Nice to hear your voice again. I thought you'd want to

know Carlton has finally accepted his fate and scheduled a meeting with Olivia."

Garrett grinned. "Good. I hope Olivia enjoys a challenge."

Elaine laughed softly. "That she does. She'll give Carlton a run for his money."

After a few questions about cases, Elaine got right to the point. "So when will you be back?"

"I'll probably book my flight to Seattle in the next few days. I need to get back to wrap up a few cases in person. After that…"

He heard someone gasp and spun around in his chair to see Delia standing inside the door. He'd texted her earlier to come upstairs when she could, even teasingly specifying there was no need for her to knock.

"Elaine, I need to go. I'll call you later." He didn't bother to wait for her reply.

He tossed his phone on the counter as he stood and walked toward Delia.

"Delia…"

Her eyes were bright and her face flushed. She shook her head sharply.

He reached for her arm, catching it as she swung away. "Delia, it's not what you think. Please…"

She shook him off. "I know what I heard. I get it. I really do. I knew you weren't going to be here forever."

He watched her fold herself inside, right in front of his eyes. She wrapped her arms around her waist, her lips thinned and her eyes shuttered. A polite smile graced her face. He knocked back the frustration mounting inside. He needed to explain, to make sure she knew how he felt. *Um, nice idea. You don't even know how you feel. Remember? Gage thinks you love her and you can't even admit it to yourself.* He shut his critic down and looked at Delia. He meant to talk to her and he would.

159

"Delia, please come in. Let me explain."

She hesitated, her arms tight around her. At that moment, a family turned down the hall, two boys jostling each other along the way. Delia glanced between him and them before taking a step through the door and closing it behind her. She walked past him to stand by the windows. She didn't look his way.

Garrett marshaled his courage. He was the master of words when it came to arguing his point in court. Yet, right now, he was floundering, struggling to find a way to explain. He kept thinking it should be simple. His highly perceptive brother was convinced he was in love. Usually, Garrett trusted Gage's judgment implicitly, but he had zero experience with love. He liked things to be clear, to be straightforward. His feelings were a messy muddle. Every time he thought about being away from Delia, his chest felt hollow. Yet, whenever he considered actually speaking his feelings aloud, fear washed through him. He was no good at this. He'd never thought he was cut out for serious relationships. He liked to be in control, to manage things. He didn't know how to manage this.

He walked to the windows. Delia stared ahead. He wanted to pull her into his arms, but she was distant. He took a breath, his eyes traveling over the now familiar view.

"I'm not sure how long I'll be in Seattle, but I have to go back. I've ignored my work longer than I should have. I was hoping maybe we could talk about…"

Delia cut him off, her eyes bright and her cheeks flushed. "Talk about what? You have your life in Seattle, and mine is here. I knew that from day one. It's okay." She whirled away from the window and started pacing back and forth in front of the bed.

He clenched his jaw. She wasn't even giving him a chance to explain.

"Maybe it's okay with you, but it's not with me. I didn't

expect this to happen. I came up here after a winning a shitty case in court. I just needed to get away and think. And then, well…" He paused, a jolt of lust coursing through him at the mere thought of the first time he kissed her. He gulped in air. He needed to stay on track somehow.

"It took a little time, but I've figured out what to do about work. I need to focus on something other than corporate cases. I already have a plan. I'm going to route all the corporate referrals to the other attorneys in my practice and start taking cases for non-profits and consultation. I don't have it completely hammered out, but I was hoping to find a way to go back and forth between Seattle and Diamond Creek until the dust settles. If I can get enough work up here, I can sell my partnership to some of the newer attorneys—the ones who have the energy and drive to keep it going."

Delia's arms were still crossed, but her expression softened slightly, the shutters lifting on her eyes if only a little. It occurred to him he was avoiding the hard part of this conversation. He was focusing on work and tiptoeing around their relationship. Because that's what it was—a relationship.

He walked to her side. She kept pacing, so he paced alongside her and dredged up the last of his nerve. "Delia, this is all new to me. I know I'm blowing it. I don't want us to end. I don't know how it's going to shake out, but I want to try to make this work. I've never done this…this relationship thing. If I could wave a magic wand and somehow sort out my life in Seattle without leaving your side, I would. I absolutely would. I'd love it if you could come with me. I'll fly up here every weekend while I'm there if you'll just give me a chance to show you how much you matter."

She came to an abrupt stop and turned to face him. "Garrett…I don't know if I can do this."

"I know. I'm not asking you to make any promises. I'm just asking you to let us see where this goes."

His heart battered against his rib cage. He waited. The room was so quiet, he could hear the soft rush of her breath before she closed the distance between them.

"Okay… I'm not so sure it's a good idea, but I can't say no. Not right now."

# CHAPTER 19

*D*elia's pulse raced. She was caught in the tides of desire and emotion. She meant what she said— she couldn't turn away from what they had. Yet, it didn't change the muddled reality of their situation. She heard Garrett's words—that he wanted a chance to make this work. But he still had an entire life in Seattle. She couldn't help but wonder if he'd change his mind once he got back home. She could only guess at how different his world there was from here. Diamond Creek's only claim to worldly came from its breathtaking beauty and world-class wilderness.

Garrett's hand threaded into her hair, shivers chasing in the wake of his touch. She looked up to find his eyes on her —dark and compelling. He spoke her name—a gruff whisper—before his lips crashed against hers. There were kisses and then there were Garrett's kisses. He fit his mouth over hers—hot, hungry and demanding. She dove into the sensations crashing through her.

He broke away from her lips, fisting his hand in her hair and exposing her throat. His lips, teeth and tongue traced a path down her throat and sent hot shivers coursing through her. Time dissolved into the blur of desire. His body was hot against hers—against the door, spinning across the room. Clothes were torn off. She found herself grasping the edge of the counter, her hands clenching and unclenching as Garrett teased her slick folds with his fingers. She was dripping with desire, desperate for more. He drove her closer and closer. He cupped her bottom with his hand as she arched back into him.

*"Garrett...please..."*

Her voice was raspy, her throat raw.

Suddenly, he slid a finger into her channel and she gasped in relief. Pushing back into his touch, another finger joined, stretching and stroking. Pleasure streaked through her, dancing just out of reach. She pushed her hips into his touch—begging for more. She felt the brush of his cock against her skin. His fingers slipped away, and his cock nudged at her entrance. He went still. She arched back, calling his name. His palm slid up her back, strong and sure, and laced in her hair. The anticipation nearly drove her mad while he held still, just the head of his cock resting in her entrance. Her channel throbbed.

In a swift surge, he seated himself in her, driving deep and hard. Her breath broke on a raw gasp before he started a cycle of long, slow, relentless strokes. Without the counter under her hands and Garrett's grip on her hips, she'd have fallen as she tumbled headlong into the fire licking its way through her. Deep strokes, his hand tugging on her hair, the feel of his cock full and hard inside of her, every breath and beat of her heart another pulse of pleasure. He reached around and with a quick stroke of his thumb across her clit, the pressure let loose, unwinding wave after wave of sharp pleasure. His guttural cry followed hers as she felt him go taut before he shuddered against her.

His hand loosened in her hair and slid down her back

slowly. He dropped a kiss on her spine before he straightened and stepped back, immediately lifting her in his arms and carrying her into the shower with him. After a steaming shower, Garrett tugged her with him to lie down.

"It's still light out." She couldn't say why, but it felt silly to lounge in bed. Or perhaps her vulnerable, ever-hopeful heart experienced a beat of hesitation. The intimacy of it gave her pause. But then she saw his eyes—that navy gaze was wide open. What she saw there took her breath away. His mouth hooked in an almost-boyish grin.

"Just for a little while. I'm still recovering," he said, gesturing to his shoulder. Which, at this point, was quite colorful. As bruises were wont to do, they had darkened as he healed. She giggled and allowed herself to be tugged into bed with him. They lay propped on the pillows while the sun finished its bow, the curtain of dusk following its last glorious burst of orange, red and gold streaking the sky above the mountains and shimmering on the water in the bay.

\* \* \*

GARRETT WATCHED Delia collect their scattered clothing. She wore one of the oversized robes from the room. It nearly swallowed her. She'd tied her hair up with loose curls escaping around her face. His heart clenched. Somehow, he had to pull himself together and get back to Seattle, so he could return here as soon as possible.

His phone buzzed on the nightstand. He snagged it and saw a text from Gage. He suddenly remembered he was supposed to meet Gage downstairs for a few beers.

He glanced up at Delia. "How about dinner downstairs?"

She shook out her blouse and looked up.

"I told Gage I'd meet him for a few beers. Maybe you

could call up and see if Marley wants to join us? I'm starving."

Such a simple request and he couldn't bear it if she said no. She nodded while she put her blouse on. Meanwhile, his mind whirred over how he could persuade her to go with him to Seattle. He didn't have the details of anything hammered out, but he knew without a doubt, he wanted to wring every possible moment of time with Delia before he had to return to Seattle.

* * *

THE SUN FELL in a slant across the bed, warming Delia. She came awake slowly. Garrett was spooned behind her with his hand curled under one of her breasts and his legs tangled with hers. She smiled to herself. Last night had been the kind of night she'd wished for whenever she let herself hope for love. But those faded dreams hadn't been specific. She'd simply wanted a good man, a man who fit into her world and who loved her and Nick. Born and raised in a small town on the wild coast of Alaska didn't lend itself to a life familiar to many. She valued the closeness of her family and friends, living in a community where trust mattered and where the occasional nosiness of neighbors was the flip side of the coin when you knew those neighbors would always drop anything to help.

They'd had a long, lazy dinner in the restaurant with Marley and Gage. Her father had joined them for a little while, bringing Nick along. Nick had crawled under the booth and climbed up between Gage and Garrett. After dinner turned to a casual game of cards, Garrett had taught him how to play rummy, his arm casually curled over Nick's shoulder. A few glasses of wine sloughed off her tendency to worry, which so often prevented her from enjoying herself fully. After her father headed off with a sleepy Nick, she'd tumbled into bed with Garrett.

Now, her hopes and dreams were Garrett specific. At the moment, she batted away her worry. Because it would have its chance to run laps in her mind later when Garrett flew to Seattle and uncertainty engulfed them. For now, she savored the moment. She felt Garrett's breathing alter slightly. He mumbled into her hair before his lips landed on her neck. He slid a hand down the curve of her hip. She felt his body tighten into a shivering stretch behind her before he relaxed against her again.

Sometime later after they were showered and she was about to head downstairs to work, she made a decision. Whatever happened, Garrett had to know how she felt before he left. He was seated at the kitchen table, scrolling through emails on his laptop. When she said his name, he glanced up.

She took a deep breath, gathering her courage. "I thought maybe you should know something."

His eyes held hers. He arched a brow. "Okay?"

She twisted her hands together. "I know you're leaving soon, so I thought you should know…I think I'm falling in love with you." Her words flew out forcefully, unvarnished and raw. Her heart pounded wildly, and she felt simultane-ously terrified and relieved—terrified to speak her feelings aloud and relieved not to keep them tucked inside anymore.

Garrett's eyes widened and his jaw went slack. "Delia…I…"

She could tell by the look on his face he had no idea what to say. Strangely, she wasn't upset she'd shared her feelings. There was no sense to hiding them. She took a breath. "I didn't mean to startle you. I just thought I might as well tell you. You're leaving, so it didn't seem to make much sense to hide how I felt."

Garrett's eyes were wide. He barely moved, but he nodded his head slowly. "Delia, I don't know what to say…"

Suddenly, she couldn't stand to wait while he fumbled his way through *not* telling her he loved her. She walked swiftly to his side and kissed him quickly. "It's okay. I just had to tell you." She all but ran out of the room on the way out, her heart pounding so loudly, she could barely hear anything else.

# CHAPTER 20

*G*arrett tossed his briefcase on his desk and put his hands on his hips, spinning in a slow circle in his office. He'd spent more time here than he had at his home—a rather sad reminder of his life. He'd spent a fortune on a high-rise apartment and all he ever did was sleep there. His office was pristine, which was not its usual state. He worked in long stretches and tended to leave papers and coffee cups all over the place. He took a deep breath and tried to focus.

There was a sharp knock on his door before it opened. He turned to see Elaine standing there. He strode to her and gave her a quick hug. She smiled broadly. Elaine was all efficiency, even in her appearance. Simple navy suits with a white blouse were practically a uniform for her. Her white hair was kept in a short, sleek cut. Her brown eyes were bright behind her round glasses. She got right to business.

"Good to have you back. Shall we review your schedule?"

Garrett ran a hand through his hair and eyed Elaine. "How about we start with an update?"

A while later, Elaine sat across from him, her lips pursed. "I don't know how I feel about this, Garrett. While I must admit, I think it's best for you to find a change of pace, I'm getting the feeling you won't be my boss for much longer. I'll miss working for you."

Garrett's throat was tight. He flipped a pen back and forth between his fingers. "I don't intend to quit practicing in Seattle completely, Elaine. As far as I'm concerned, I'd love for you to keep working for me. Things will definitely be different though. You won't have to deal with any more Carltons. I've had my fill of that."

Elaine grinned. "I occasionally enjoy sparring with Carlton. So fill me in on how you plan to do this?"

"We'll funnel all the corporate cases to the other partners. Becca's already filling up my email with referrals for bleeding heart cases. I keep telling her I'm not cut out for prosecution, so she's finding me all kinds of consulting work for non-profits. Once I get things more settled here, I need to get my law license set up in Alaska. I don't know how much work I can get there to start. It's easy enough to work from a distance these days. The flight to Seattle is only four hours. If you agree to stay on for me, you'll run the show here, and I'll come down when I need to."

Elaine tilted her head to the side and smiled softly. "Sounds like you've worked it all out. So tell me, who is she?"

Garrett laughed. "Damn, you cut right to it, Elaine. What gave you the idea there was a woman involved?"

"I actually didn't guess. I might have if I'd seen you, but it was Becca. She stopped by to pick up your mail a few times and mentioned she thought you'd finally met your match."

"Ah, should've guessed. What did Becca have to say?"

Elaine smiled softly. "Not much really. I think she was hoping for the best. She's bossy, you know. For once, she wasn't telling me what she thought you should do."

Garrett chuckled. "Probably because I already asked her what to do."

"She didn't mention her name. She just said she thought you were in love."

"Delia. That's her name." His heart clenched at merely saying her name aloud.

"Is Becca right?"

Garrett arched a brow. "About what?"

"Do you love her?"

His heart thumped, almost painfully, in his chest. He'd yet to dredge up the nerve to say the word. But he knew it to be true. His mind replayed the moment at the lodge when Delia told him she thought she was falling in love with him. He'd frozen and fumbled that completely.

He met Elaine's eyes and sighed.

Her eyes widened slightly. "So you love her, but you don't have the nerve to tell her?"

He groaned and rolled his head back. "That obvious, huh?"

"I've been around a lot longer than you. Been there myself. Want some advice?"

"This will be the second time since I met Delia I've asked someone to tell me what to do."

Elaine grinned. "I'll keep it simple: don't be stupid. If you must, practice."

"Practice what?"

"That word."

"Love?"

"Keep saying it. Eventually it will get easier."

* * *

DELIA PUSHED through the lodge door into the cold, starry night. She was the last one to leave tonight, as had been the case almost every night since Garrett returned to Seattle. As she approached her car, she stopped and looked up at the sky. Stars stretched across the sky—a glittering glory of patterns. She spun around slowly. Her breath caught when she spied the shimmer of northern lights above the mountains across the bay. They were faint, but even then they awed her. She remembered nights when she was a little girl when her mother would wake her to go outside and see the dancing lights. She took a deep breath, savoring the biting air.

Tears pricked at the back of her eyes. Garrett's absence hit her with a sharp pang. He'd been gone a week now. He called every morning and every night and texted her throughout the day. She was entirely unaccustomed to the kind of attention he bestowed upon her, even from a distance. It was both endearing and unsettling—and she missed him so. Her father had pointed out this morning that she was working too hard, but it was the only way she could manage herself. Work grounded her and helped pass the time.

Without it, her mind ran laps on the track of its worries. She couldn't help but think that once Garrett settled in at home he'd change his mind.

She shook her head sharply and took another gulp of air before she finished crossing the parking lot. The snow crunched under her feet. She took one last look at the sky before climbing in her car and driving home alone in the quiet night.

The next morning, Delia woke to the sound of Nick's footsteps pounding down the hallway. There was a loud banging on her door.

"Mom! I missed the bus!"

She kicked the covers off and leapt out of bed. "Coming!"

She took a three-minute shower and tossed on her

clothes. She raced into the kitchen, grabbing her purse off the counter. "Ready?" she asked, glancing to Nick. "Where's your granddad by the way?"

Nick threw his backpack over his shoulder. "He said he had to leave early for some deliveries at the lodge."

After a swift drive on icy roads, Delia watched Nick jog into school right as the bell rang. She leaned her head against the steering wheel and sighed. Mornings like this made her feel as if she was always one step behind, skidding along the rails of her life barely keeping her balance. She sat up and leaned back, debating whether she should head to the lodge now, or go later. She knew if she went in this morning, Harry would roll his eyes and tell her he was worried about her. Though Garrett was calling every day, more than once, she still didn't really know what his plans were beyond a vague idea.

She jumped when someone knocked on her window. She turned to find Ginger waving at her on the other side of the window, her breath billowing in the cold air. Delia hit the button and her window whirred down.

"Let's get coffee," Ginger said by way of greeting.

"I should probably go to work."

Ginger arched a brow. "Seriously? You don't need to go to work this early. Marley said you've been working yourself to death and hardly talk to anyone."

Delia chewed her lip and sighed. "Okay, okay. Let's get coffee. Misty Mountain?"

"Of course! If it were summer, I'd say Red Truck Coffee, but that's a no go in the winter. Meet you there in a few." Ginger whirled away and jogged across the street to her car.

A few minutes later, Delia walked into Misty Mountain. Ginger was waiting for her just inside the door. She hooked her hand through Delia's elbow. "Coffee's on me."

The tight feeling started to ease in Delia's chest as they

waited in line. Misty Mountain was bustling with the soft hum of conversation. The scent of fresh baked goods drifted through the café. She glanced around, her eyes coasting over familiar faces. The sharp ache in her heart from Garrett's absence softened slightly.

Moments later, they sat down with coffees and pastries. Ginger took a sip of coffee and gave her an assessing look. "So, how's the long-distance thing going?"

"What do you mean?"

Ginger rolled her eyes. "Oh my God, don't be ridiculous. Here, let me spell it out. You and Garrett are in a relationship, even if you don't want to say it out loud. According to Marley, Garrett is only down in Seattle long enough to sort out his practice and then he'll be back. As far as I'm concerned, you hit the jackpot. He's sexy as hell, rich, and heads over heels in love with you from everything I've heard. Meanwhile, you're running scared."

Delia's stomach felt hollow, as if she was falling. "I'm not…"

"Yes, you are. I don't blame you. You've been doing this alone for so long, I imagine it's pretty hard to think about believing in someone else. Of all people, you know I understand. But it sounds like Garrett is the real deal, even if he didn't fit what you had in mind." Ginger's voice softened and she reached across the table to give Delia's hand a squeeze.

Delia took a sip of coffee and traced the edge of the table. Ginger would certainly understand why it might be difficult to trust. She'd married her college sweetheart only to have him stay rather busy with his wandering eye. Ginger's warm, sunny and trusting disposition had absorbed the blow of a bitter divorce. In the years since, she'd yet to take the plunge into the dating pool. That didn't stop her from sharing her opinions about the love lives of her friends. She was overprotective to a fault, so if she was encouraging Delia to be open to the possibilities Garrett represented, then Delia might want to sit up and take notice. If her relentlessly hopeful heart could be heard over the din of the spinning tracks of worry in her mind, maybe she could consider it.

"He definitely wasn't what I imagined. Not that I'm complaining, but that's part of the problem. He could have his pick of women. He's a wealthy corporate lawyer. How the hell did I end up with him? Why would he want me?"

"If you focus on the surface of his life, you're going to drive yourself crazy. So what if he's a corporate lawyer? Gage is his brother, and Gage is an awesome guy. Why wouldn't his brother be halfway decent too? And stop acting like you're not worth Garrett's attention. You're gorgeous. You're just a busy, single mom who forgot how cute you were. Working yourself to the bone doesn't help."

Delia took a gulp of coffee and glanced out the window before turning back to meet Ginger's gaze. "Maybe you have a point. I just don't know how this is going to work out. He's down in Seattle doing his lawyer thing. He says he'll be back, but I don't know when. What if…"

Ginger cut her off. "Don't start with the 'what ifs.' You'll drive yourself completely insane. I'm not saying there's a guarantee you and Garrett will work out, but how about you try to stop manufacturing things in your head that haven't even happened? What's happening now?"

"Well, he calls me…"

"How often?"

"In the morning and at night."

"He calls you not once, but twice a day, and you're freaking out. Do you know how many women would pay good money to have someone call even just once a day?" Ginger was incredulous. She sat back and crossed her arms, glaring at Delia.

"Ginger, it's not that simple. Don't get me wrong, I think I'm freaking out because I still can't quite believe it."

Ginger's glare faded and she grinned softly. "Maybe I'm being a teensy bit too hard on you. Since I haven't been lucky in love, I get a little crazy if I think my friends are letting a good thing pass them by."

## CHAPTER 21

"What the hell do you mean we should consider settling? This is bullshit. I want to talk to Garrett. Now!"

Garrett stood by Elaine's desk outside the conference room. Olivia was in there getting a taste of Carlton's behavior. Garrett shook his head slowly. The door flew open and slammed against the wall. Carlton stomped, literally stomped, to Garrett's side. "Did you hear that? This won't work. I need…"

Garrett took a step back and buttoned his suit jacket. "Carlton, Ms. Brooks is a damn good attorney. You should appreciate the fact she's willing to tell you the truth. You can't fight everyone and certainly not just because they happened to purchase health insurance from your company and had the gall to use it."

Olivia walked out of the conference room. She was a younger version of Elaine at a glance—navy suit, sleek hair cropped close to her head, and brown eyes. She appeared entirely unruffled by Carlton's outburst. She caught

Garrett's eye with a barely perceptible smile. He nodded as she continued to her office, ignoring Carlton completely.

Carlton cleared his throat, and Garrett turned back to him. "If you're back to work, why can't you handle my cases?" Carlton asked, his tone bullish.

"Because I don't plan to continue corporate work. I'm scaling back my practice here and will be relocating to Alaska sometime soon."

Carlton's mouth dropped before he snapped it shut. "Are you crazy? You're leaving a lot of money on the table. Why would you walk away from corporate work?"

Garrett stared at Carlton for a few beats and abruptly decided he had nothing to lose by being honest. "Because I've had my fill. I'd like to do more work that matters."

Carlton sputtered, his face turning red. He started yammering on about why various cases mattered. Garrett lost patience quickly.

"My decision's been made. Like I told you, you're welcome to take your business elsewhere, but Ms. Brooks is an excellent attorney. You're lucky to have her."

At that, Garrett turned away and strode into his office. He checked the urge to slam the door and closed it slowly. He sat down at his desk and spun around in his chair to look out the window. His office was in a high-rise building in downtown Seattle. Puget Sound was visible in the distance. The sky was slate gray and a soft mist fell.

He missed Delia—every day. Phone calls and texts weren't enough. He couldn't shake the feeling that Delia didn't quite believe he'd return to Diamond Creek. Meanwhile, he was up to his ears in work here. Winding down his corporate work was, well, work. He was finding it hard to focus on anything new because he wanted to be able to close this chapter of his life.

Restless, he stood abruptly and grabbed his raincoat. Once outside, he threaded through the other pedestrians on his way to Becca's office. Her office was only a few blocks away from his, but it felt like an entirely different world. It was crowded and noisy in the waiting room. When he finally made it through the crowd to the back, he found Becca in her office glaring at Aidan McNamara.

Aidan was an old friend of Gage's and a former Navy SEAL colleague. He ran a private security firm in Seattle and occasionally crossed paths with them in his work. Becca stood in front of him, hands on her hips, her blue eyes snapping and her mouth twisted with a frown.

"Just because you think I need to pay better attention to security doesn't give you the right to show up here unannounced."

Aidan towered over Becca. He towered over most everyone, to be honest. He crossed his arms and eyed her. "You may not like it, but Gage would never let me forget it if I didn't check on you after hearing something like this. The woman you're representing is involved with a dangerous man. You need to consider some safety measures…"

Becca threw her hands up. "I specialize in cases involving domestic violence. Almost every case I handle involves a dangerous man!"

Becca hadn't noticed Garrett yet, but Aidan had. He nodded in Garrett's direction.

Garrett looked between them. "Becca, what the hell is going on?"

Becca turned to him, her eyes flashing with annoyance. "My job is going on. That's all this is. I don't know why…" she paused and waved a hand toward Aidan "…Aidan thinks he needs to help me."

Aidan turned to Garrett. "A buddy of mine who does some security for the courthouse gave me a heads up that the perp on one of Becca's cases is a special kind of crazy. I stopped by to give Becca a heads up." Aidan shifted his gaze to Becca. Contrary to what you think, I was only trying to help."

Becca turned away and sat down at her desk. Her gaze bounced to Garrett. "What brings you here?"

"Came by to see if you wanted to grab some lunch." He waited a beat, assessing her level of irritation. Becca was a brilliant prosecutor with the softest of hearts underneath her prickly exterior. If Aidan was concerned enough to stop by and check on Becca, there was probably reason to worry. But if there was one thing Garrett knew very well about his twin sister, it was that she responded to pressure by generally going in the opposite direction. He elected to gloss over the moment. He nodded in Aidan's direction. "You could join us if you'd like."

"Did I mention I could go yet?" Becca asked, her tone heavy with sarcasm.

Garrett shook his head with a grin. "No, but you need to eat and I'd bet money you didn't bother with breakfast. Come on, let's go grab something at the Thai place next door."

Becca grumbled, but she stood and grabbed an umbrella and her purse. Aidan held the door as they passed through. The rain had picked up in the few minutes since Garrett had entered Becca's office, so they dashed through the showers and into the restaurant. Once they were seated, Becca turned to Aidan.

"Have you heard Garrett's news?"

Aidan shook his raincoat out and hung it on his chair before sitting down. "Heard from Gage you might be moving to Diamond Creek."

Becca caught Garrett's eyes. "Might?" she asked archly.

Garrett shifted uncomfortably in his chair. He was saved from having to answer immediately when a waiter arrived. After they ordered, Becca got right back on point.

"How does Delia feel about this 'might be moving to Alaska' situation?"

Garrett rolled his eyes. "Nothing's changed. I'm just not sure when I'm going. I can't walk away from my practice here, so I'm working on getting cases transferred and finishing up on a few. Once that's taken care of and I've got my feet under me for the move, it'll happen."

Aidan angled his head and grinned. "First Gage and now you."

"What do you mean?"

"Like Gage, I figured you'd stay single forever. Next thing I know, you go for a visit to Diamond Creek and suddenly you're in love."

"Maybe you should take a trip there someday soon," Garrett countered.

Aidan bit back a laugh, and Becca glared at him before turning back to Garrett with an arch of her brow.

Garrett rolled his shoulders, still experiencing a lingering ache from his fall on the mountain. While he missed Delia like crazy, every time the word 'love' came up, he got uncomfortable. He didn't know what to make of it, so he ignored it.

"Delia's not the only reason I'm moving. I'm just, I don't know, burned out on corporate work here. Alaska's a breath of fresh air, literally. I'll be keeping a small footprint here with my practice though." *Damn, you managed to sidestep that one. You can hardly stand to be without Delia, but if anyone points out what that might mean, you act like it's no big deal.* He ignored his taunting mind.

Becca's gaze bounced from him to Aidan. "Garrett hasn't figured out yet that he might have to admit Delia means a lot to him."

Aidan chuckled, while Garrett bristled and bit his tongue. Becca must have sensed his frustration because she let the topic drop, moving on to ask him about a few of the referrals she'd made to him. After they finished eating and stood to leave, Garrett's curiosity was piqued when he saw Aidan's gaze linger on Becca. When Aidan said goodbye at the door, Becca's cheeks flushed. Garrett walked with Becca back to her office. Once they were in her office away from the bedlam in the waiting area, Becca turned to him.

"Don't dance around this thing with Delia," she said pointedly.

"Why do you think I'm dancing around something? I'm in the middle of uprooting my life and…"

"I know that. But every time someone points out the obvious, you go sideways and act like it's nothing. I'm just saying if that's how it looks from here that might be how it looks and sounds to Delia. The way you talk about it, you just need a change of pace and Delia happens to be there. I think it's true you seriously need a change of pace, but if Delia means as much as to you as I'm guessing, you might want to make sure she doesn't end up feeling like an afterthought."

Garrett's throat tightened. "Becca, how much more do I need to do for her to know how much she means to me?"

Becca's eyes softened and she sat down at her desk with a sigh. "Trust me, I don't doubt how much she means to you. I know you better than I'd like sometimes. You're scared to death. It's like you're afraid to really commit even though you're doing all the right things on the surface. You know I understand how scary it is to fall on your face when it comes to love. Did you forget my fiancée called off our wedding two days before it was supposed to happen? I'm bitter, but you're not. All I'm saying is don't be afraid to express yourself. You need to be able to make sure she knows how you feel."

Garrett took a breath and nodded slowly. "I get it. Elaine told me I have to practice saying it."

Becca arched a brow. "Saying what?"

"That I love Delia." He had to force the words out of his mouth, an unfamiliar anxiety and vulnerability tightening his chest. He was accustomed to feeling in control, and when it came to Delia, he tended to feel off kilter and uncertain—a feeling he didn't appreciate.

Becca grinned. "Elaine knows best."

At that, Garrett turned to leave. On his way out, he paused and glanced back at Becca. "I know it's part of your job every day, but you might want to heed Aidan's advice and take some extra precautions with that case he mentioned."

Becca nodded. "I know he was trying to help. I'll give him a call to find out what he knows."

"Thanks. Let me know if you need anything."

Garrett made his way out back into the damp afternoon. Instead of returning to his office, he texted Elaine that he'd be in tomorrow morning and headed home. Once there, he found himself restless. He ended up spending hours working on a few legal briefs. Late that night, he stood by the windows staring out across the city, its lights a blurry glimmer in the rainy darkness. He turned from the view and carefully put away the takeout he'd ordered. He washed his single plate and fork and placed them in the drying rack. His kitchen was quiet and stark, void of the warm feeling he associated with the kitchen at Last Frontier Lodge. He imagined a kitchen in a home with Delia. It likely wouldn't be pristine as his so often was because he rarely used it. He tried to recall if he'd ever cooked a meal here and couldn't come up with a sole memory of such an event. With a sigh, he walked out of the kitchen and flicked the light off.

* * *

DELIA STARED out the windows of the lodge early one morning. On the heels of another late night, she'd rolled out of bed after a restless night of sleep. She'd arrived at the restaurant before anyone else and started baking. With everything in the oven, her time was idle now until the restaurant opened for breakfast. The sun was making its way up behind the mountains, its presence heralded by streaks of lavender in the winter sky. The days in Alaska flipped swiftly. After the dark months over the holidays, it was now almost technically spring and the sun was rising earlier every day. Spring was slow to come in Alaska with the snow lingering well into May some years. She watched a snowshoe hare bound across the snow in front of the deck at the foot of the ski slopes. The hare covered the distance swiftly and paused by the corner of the deck to nibble on a few shoots of green coming up through the snow.

A magpie burst out of the nearby trees and swooped down over the hare, chattering madly. As the magpie flew to land on the deck, the sun crested from behind the mountains, its rays catching on the iridescent wings. Delia grinned as the magpie meandered along the deck, curiously inspecting a pair of skis left by the railing. Garrett wandered through her thoughts. It had been almost a month since he'd left now. He still called every day, but his texts were less frequent. She was worried her fears were coming to fruition. Garrett was back in Seattle and the pulsing beats of emotion and desire she'd felt with him were probably nothing more than a distant memory to him. She took a breath, letting it out slowly. She should appreciate what she'd had with him, even if it faded with time. Garrett had reminded her she could experience passion and more.

She turned away and shut thoughts of Garrett out of her mind. The main door to the lodge opened and seconds later Harry walked into the restaurant. Delia got to work with him, helping get all the tables ready for the morning crowd as wait staff arrived over the next few minutes. Before she knew it, the restaurant was almost full with guests filling up on breakfast before heading up on the slopes. The bustle kept Delia's mind focused throughout the day.

Marley stopped by Delia's office late that afternoon. "Hey there," Marley said, her auburn hair swishing in its ponytail as she leaned her head around the door.

"Hey, how's it going?"

Marley shrugged, but her eyes held a gleam. "What?" Delia asked.

Marley stepped into her office and closed the door. "I'm pregnant," she whispered with a wide smile.

Delia stood and stepped around the desk, squeezing Marley in a quick hug. "Congratulations! This is so exciting!" She took a step back, her eyes coasting over Marley. "You can't be too far along because you're definitely not showing."

Marley kept grinning. "Hardly at all. I can't believe I'm telling anyone, but I have to say something. I missed my period this month and took a pregnancy test this morning."

Delia chuckled. "Have you even told Gage?"

Marley nodded quickly. "He's ecstatic." She sat down with a satisfied sigh on the small couch in Delia's office.

Delia couldn't help but remember that damn couch held a memory with Garrett that made her blush. She shoved the memory away and focused on Marley. When she'd gotten pregnant, she hadn't had the chance to share the joy with anyone. Though she'd never questioned her choice to have Nick, her pregnancy had been unplanned and unwelcome as far as Nick's father was concerned. A bitter twist in her heart caused her throat to tighten. She'd had so much hope for a chance with Garrett, and now it felt like it was slipping away. She shook her head sharply and brought her mind to the moment. Marley chattered on about planning. After a few minutes, Marley angled her head to the side and eyed Delia.

"Are you okay?" Marley asked.

Delia nodded quickly. "I'm fine."

"Fine? Uh oh. That usually means you're not fine. What's going on?"

Delia twisted a lock of hair around her finger and chewed her lip. "I think something's up with Garrett."

"What do you mean? Gage hasn't mentioned anything."

"Just that he's being vague about when he might be back and not really talking about his plans. He still calls every day, but it feels like he's not sure. I don't know if he ever was. Everything happened so fast. Maybe he confused lust with something more."

Marley slid across the couch and squeezed Delia's shoulders. "Don't go there. It won't help. Maybe you should ask him before you make assumptions like this."

Delia heard Marley's words, but it was hard to not make assumptions. She could feel the distance growing between her and Garrett—literally and metaphorically. She thought back to the afternoon before he'd left when she'd impulsively told him she thought she was falling in love with him. He'd looked frozen. At the time, she'd tried to tell herself it was just because she startled him. Now all she could think was that her silly heart got a little too hopeful. Delia fought the tears clogging her throat. "I'll try to ask him."

# CHAPTER 22

*G*arrett glanced at his watch and pushed away from his desk. It was going on ten at night, and he was still at the office. Elaine had left hours ago. He knew from the muted sounds that a few other attorneys were still here as well. There was an unhealthy pride among corporate attorneys about the grueling hours they put in at the office. The relentless pace was expected by most clients and rewarded by hefty fees. He suddenly realized he hadn't called Delia yet today. He snagged his phone off the desk and tapped her name. When she answered, her voice sounded tired. His heart clenched with worry and something else he couldn't define.

"Hey babe, how's your day been?"

"Busy. How about you?"

"Same, same."

The conversation continued lightly until Delia paused for a long beat.

"Can I ask you something?" she asked.

Garrett's stomach coiled with tension. He didn't even

know where this was going, but it didn't feel good. "Of course."

"Now you're back in Seattle, how are you feeling about us?"

Anxiety knotted in his chest. He forced himself to take a deep breath. "Good. I know it's been busy for me, but I'm sorting things out here so I can get back to you soon."

"But what does that mean? You said you wanted to give us a chance, but it doesn't seem like you have any concrete plans. I don't even know if you really want to make this work."

"Delia..."

"Garrett, I can't wait for something this vague. It felt real when you were here, but now it seems like you're not sure." Her words sped up as she talked, tightening the coil of dread inside of him. "I think we need to take a break until you know what you really want."

"Delia, please..."

"Garrett, be honest with me. You haven't even mentioned coming here for a visit, or asked me about coming down there. You don't seem to have any idea of when you'll be coming back. When will I even see you again?"

Her question felt like a punch to his gut. His mind spun. He felt out of control, inside and out. Delia was pushing him, and he didn't know how to respond. He opened his mouth, but no words came out. A sense of panic spiraled inside. He closed his eyes and took a breath. He meant to tell her he wanted to see her as soon as he could, but what he said instead was... "How about I check my calendar and see if I can get up there next weekend?"

He heard the sharp intake of Delia's breath. "You need to check your schedule?"

"I didn't mean that the way it sounded. I meant..."

"Don't bother. I can't do this."

He heard her words catch on a sob before the line clicked to silent in his ear. He immediately hit redial, but the phone range and rang.

He paced in his apartment hours later. Usually, he would savor a drink after a late night at the office. Tonight, nothing settled him. He'd tried several more times to reach Delia to no avail.

\* \* \*

DELIA FORCED herself to try to get back into the normal rhythms of her life before Garrett had upended it. She ferried Nick to his baseball practices and stayed busy with work. Marley had tried to talk to her about Garrett, but she'd waved her off. Her father's concerned glances annoyed her. A bright light through the gloom of her life came from Helen's efforts to build a relationship with Nick. Helen was gracious and respectful about checking in ahead of time before she came down for visits. Much to Delia's relief, Helen never mentioned Terry. She seemed to sincerely only want a chance to get to know her grandson. Nick soaked up her attention. Her presence in their lives, though it was occasional since she lived in Anchorage, elicited new questions from Nick about his father. Delia used the phrases she'd memorized to give him clear answers about the situation without creating false hope. The sad truth was that witnessing Nick's wish for a father rubbed at the raw absence of Garrett in her heart.

One morning she headed into Misty Mountain for coffee. Seated at a table by the windows, she pulled out her laptop and started working on monthly reports. She was deep in the middle of entering data when she felt a tap on her shoulder. She glanced up to find Ginger grinning at her.

"Hey you!" Ginger said with a quick squeeze of Delia's

shoulder before she plunked down in the empty chair across from her.

Delia saved what she was working on and closed her laptop. "Hey you too!" She tried to feel cheerful, but it was hard to sustain. Ever since she'd broken it off with Garrett, her emotions felt muted.

Ginger's gaze sobered. She set her coffee down and leaned her elbows on the table. "Marley says you called it off with Garrett."

"So what if I did?"

Ginger sighed dramatically and sat back in her chair. "You did exactly what I was worried about."

"What do you mean?"

"You let your tendency to worry make your decisions for you."

"Ginger, I didn't break it off without trying to talk to Garrett first. I asked him when he planned to see me again, and he said he had to check his calendar! I can't sit around waiting for someone who needs to schedule me into his life." Her heart thumped painfully, but she forced herself to breathe. It had been a few days, so the sharpness of the pain was dulling to an ache that didn't seem inclined to go away anytime soon.

Ginger's brows hitched up and her eyes widened. She shook her head, her glossy brown hair swinging around her shoulders. "Okay, that bites. He really said that?"

Delia nodded and took a swallow of coffee.

Ginger sighed. "Why do men have to be so reliably stupid sometimes?"

Delia shrugged. "Wish I knew. I told him not to bother. Maybe I did let my worries lead the way, but I can't get hung up on someone who's getting cold feet. Our worlds are pretty different. Diamond Creek's a far cry from Seattle. Maybe he got back and realized he missed it. I don't know."

"Marley's all worried about you. It sounds like Gage

might have talked to Garrett, but he doesn't have any more to add. Dammit. This sucks. If he does show back up around here, he'll be hearing about this bullshit from me."

Delia managed a smile through the tightness in her chest. Ginger was that kind of friend. She wouldn't hesitate to publicly humiliate anyone who hurt her friends.

"If he ever comes back here, I'm sure you'll get the chance."

Ginger pursed her lips and started to say something and stopped.

"What?"

"Oh, I was about to rant on Garrett, but I know from experience that doesn't usually help. All I can say is he didn't give me the feeling he was a jerk, so maybe he just needs a little time."

A while later, Delia drove up to the lodge, thoughts of Garrett intruding in her mind even though she tried to push them away. She missed him on a visceral level. But she had to find a way to move on. If Garrett had taught her one thing, it was that her youthful fantasies about love were lightweight to what it truly felt like to love and lose someone.

GARRETT STARED BLINDLY out his office window. The gray, misty Seattle weather suited his mood perfectly. He kept replaying his last call with Delia in his mind. *"You need to check your schedule?"* Her question echoed over and over. He mentally kicked himself again and again. He prided himself on being cool and calm under pressure. Every word he said was usually deliberate and considered before it came out of his mouth. Delia, or rather the way he felt about her, short-circuited his brain and turned on the stupid.

There was a sharp knock at his door. He swiveled around in his chair.

"Come in," he called.

Elaine stepped through the door and closed it behind her. She walked to his desk and set a few files on the edge before sitting down across from him. She crossed her legs and adjusted her glasses. Her warm brown eyes met his. She was silent long enough that he felt compelled to speak.

"What?"

She pursed her lips and tapped her fingers on the armrest of her chair. "It might be none of my business, but you need to get back on a plane to Alaska. Preferably sooner rather than later."

Garrett ran a hand through his hair. His heart squeezed painfully and his throat felt tight—a sensation that was becoming familiar. "Elaine..."

"Becca called me."

Irritation rose inside. Leave it to Becca to interfere. "Oh really?"

"Garrett, she's worried about you, and so am I. I'm not sure exactly what happened with Delia, but you're wandering around here like a lost puppy. You can barely focus on work."

He took a slow breath, trying to ease the ache in his chest. "I know. I suppose it's a damn good thing I don't have any court hearings this week."

Elaine smiled softly. "What happened?"

He shifted his shoulders, noticing the residual soreness from his fall in the snowy, dark night was almost gone. Strangely, he missed it. The pain was a reminder of Delia. "I don't know exactly. I was calling every day and she asked me to get more specific about when we'd see each other again." He threw a hand up. "Next thing I know I said the dumbest thing I could and she broke it off. Told me not to bother." He had to fight the tears that threatened. He couldn't remember feeling like this—*ever*.

Elaine nodded slowly. "What did you say?"

Garrett groaned and leaned his chin in his hand. "Told her I'd have to check my calendar."

Elaine's eyes widened. "I know you already said it, but that *really* was dumb on your part."

"Trust me, I know. I've tried to call her back, but she's not answering."

"What are you waiting for?"

"What do you mean?"

"If she's as important as she seems to be to you, you don't need to be sitting around hoping she'll answer the phone. Get on a plane and go up there. Actions speak much louder than words."

Garrett leaned back in his chair and stared at the ceiling. He tried to gather his thoughts and explain himself to Elaine, so she'd understand why he was waiting. The problem was, he had no idea himself. He couldn't seem to take action one way or another. Since the ceiling offered no answers, he brought his gaze back to Elaine.

"You think if I go up there, that'll help?"

"I think sitting here hoping she'll answer the phone definitely won't help." Elaine angled her head to the side, her gaze assessing. "I don't think I've ever had an opinion about your love life because there was never anything to have an opinion about. All I know is the look on your face when you talk about Delia is the look of someone in love. I'm getting the idea you're pretty scared of how you feel. You don't have to listen to me, but trust me when I say it's not that easy to find someone that makes you feel like that. If you want a chance, you're going to have to put yourself out there."

Garrett sighed and ran a hand through his hair again. "Okay, okay. I'll get organized here and…"

"Garrett, you don't need to organize anything. You

didn't before you left last time. At least this time, you've got most of your active cases reassigned and clients notified. I'll take care of anything else. Just go."

Elaine stood and picked up the files she'd carried with her. "Let me know your plans." At that, she briskly left his office.

He replayed their conversation, trying to pinpoint his discomfort. *She's right. You're scared. If you can't get up the nerve to face Delia, you might as well admit you're giving up.* At that taunt from his inner critic, he swore and stood.

He didn't even bother going home. He left messages for Becca and Gage on his way to the airport.

# CHAPTER 23

*D*elia sat at her desk, trying to stay focused on ordering supplies for the month. This was her first year managing the restaurant, so sometimes she felt a little lost. The winter had turned out much busier than she'd anticipated. Fortunately, Gage was as new to this as she was and was patient with her missteps. She felt like she was flying by the seat of her pants sometimes. One way or another, she'd pulled together enough supplies and settled into a rhythm. With spring around the corner, she wasn't certain how to plan. She had access to her mother's old records from the days her mother ran the lodge restaurant, but those records were over twenty years old. This first winter since Gage had reopened Last Frontier Lodge had exceeded the busiest season the lodge ever had back in the day when his grandparents owned it.

With Last Frontier Lodge being the only ski lodge on the southern Kenai Peninsula in Alaska, she had little for comparison. Given that the restaurant had a steady flow of local customers, she was trying to use those numbers to help her plan for the spring. Gage intended to keep the

lodge open year-round. He'd already developed relation-
ships with some local guide businesses for referrals. He'd
partnered with the Winters brothers who ran a fishing and
guiding business in Diamond Creek, along with Trey
Holden who led flightseeing tours into the backcountry.
Gage hoped to turn the lodge into more than a ski lodge.
His relentless work ethic had paid dividends this winter, so
Delia figured she'd better be ready for a busy summer. This
would be an entirely new endeavor for the lodge. When
Delia had grown up tagging along with her mother in the
lodge kitchen, the lodge closed every summer.

She completed her orders and switched over to updating
monthly reports. There was a knock at her door. She
absently called out for whomever it was to come in without
looking up.

"Delia."

Garrett's voice was low, gravelly and unmistakable. Her
heart nearly leapt out of her chest. She whipped her head
up. The sight of him was so good, a flare of joy raced
through her. She had to force herself to stay calm. She
wasn't going to make a fool of herself. He looked tired. His
hair was mussed as if he'd run a hand through it a few too
many times. He wore a suit jacket and button down shirt,
both of which were rumpled. His blue eyes were weary and
wary at once.

"Garrett. I, uh, didn't know you were coming."

He shrugged. "Me neither. I decided I'd just come up
again." He paused and glanced over his shoulder when
someone called her name.

She stood and walked to the door. "Yeah?"

Harry was on his way over to her office. He paused at
the door when he saw Garrett. After quickly greeting
Garrett, he turned to Delia. "Annie called out sick again, so
if you can fill in out front in a little while, that would
be great."

"Sure. What time does her shift start?"

"Not until five. I can cover the early part, but once six hits, it's too busy for just me."

"No problem. Is she okay?"

Harry shook his head. "She has a bad cold and sounds like hell, but I'm sure she'll be fine in a few days."

His eyes bounced from Garrett to Delia again with a subtle arch of his brow. Delia knew he was wondering what was going on, but she was just as surprised as him. She shrugged, and Harry turned away with a wave.

Delia closed the door behind him and stepped back to her desk. She leaned her hips against her desk and crossed her arms, trying to contain the emotions surging through her. She'd missed Garrett so. She'd done her damnedest to block it out, but she'd failed completely. Every night, she fell asleep thinking about him and spent most of her days batting thoughts of him away. She felt like she was playing a game of dodge ball in her mind. To have him standing here in front of her set her body to humming. He was so damn sexy that even tired and rumpled, he took her breath away and sent heat sliding through her veins.

Garrett was quiet, his eyes locked to hers. His shoulders rose and fell with a deep breath. He moved suddenly, closing the short distance between them in two strides. Her breath caught and her pulse rocketed. He threaded a hand into her hair and brought his mouth to hers before she could think to hesitate. Once his lips landed, she was lost. His first touch was soft, almost a question. When she arched into him, his tongue traced her lips before delving inside. Sensation took over and she gasped into his mouth—a gasp of relief and pure need at once. His kiss seared her through —hot, wet, and deep.

He tore free and his lips traveled down her neck in a sizzling path. Shudders wracked her body. His free hand slid down her back, his touch strong and sure. He stepped into the cradle of her hips, and she felt the heat of his hard shaft like a brand against her. Unable to keep herself from arching against him, she moaned as hot, liquid need pooled between her thighs and her sex clenched with want. She scrambled for purchase in her mind, trying to drag herself out of the madness. She managed to choke out his name.

He stilled and lifted his head. His blue eyes were nearly impossible to look away from. She wanted to just forget herself and let her body's needs rule. But she couldn't. She had to pull herself together.

"We can't start like this," she said, gesturing between them. Her body protested, but she ignored the need throbbing through her.

He nodded slowly. "I'm sorry. I just…" His eyes looked pained as he took a shuddering breath. "I missed you. That's all."

She could feel his heartbeat under her palm that had landed on his chest. It pounded fast and hard, in tune with her own. "I missed you too." Her words slipped out without her permission. She wanted to grab them back. She didn't want to be as vulnerable as she felt with him. She couldn't put her heart on the line if all he meant to be was temporary.

She looked up at him and gulped in air. "Why are you here, Garrett?"

"Isn't that obvious?"

"No, not really. Last time we talked, you didn't seem to know anything permanent about your plans. What's changed?"

When he was silent for a long moment, she purposefully pulled her hand away from his chest even though it took all of her willpower. She shimmied out from between him and the desk and moved quickly around to the other side. Putting a desk between them might help her keep her head clear. His eyes tracked her movements.

She felt bereft at the forced separation from him—just this tiny moment and all she wanted was him. Again.

"You haven't answered my question."

He ran a hand through his hair and sighed. "Nothing changed to begin with for me. I'm still sorting through things with my practice and have transferred most of my cases. Before you stopped talking to me, I had already applied for my law license here."

Her heart leapt at that, hope hollering to be heard. She couldn't put her finger on it, but it wasn't that she needed to know exactly when he'd be in Alaska more full-time. She didn't expect him to uproot his life for her. What she wanted was to know what she meant to him. When they were skin to skin, their hearts beating as one and their bodies entwined, she knew what she felt. But in the less intense moments, she sensed Garrett wasn't sure, that he just might walk away from it all because it wasn't tidy to care that deeply for someone. The emotional knots she felt were anything but tidy. She felt tossed like a kite in the winds of her emotions and didn't like how deeply he affected her and what he meant to her. If she was going to put her heart on the line, she couldn't do it alone.

She forced herself to take a breath, trying to gather herself together. She made a swift decision. If she expected him to put himself out there, she at least needed to show the courage she wanted from him.

"Garrett, I love you." As soon as the words came out, she panicked even though she'd almost said them once already. She'd spent so many years making sure she didn't make a fool of herself again, the way she had with Terry all those years ago. Funny thing was she'd felt foolish over Terry, but her feelings had never even come close to what she felt for Garrett. She looked away and tried to slow her racing pulse. When she turned back, Garrett looked stunned and frozen. Tears clogged her throat and pricked at her eyes. She fumbled forward. "You have to understand. When I told you before I thought I was falling in love with you, I already was. I just didn't have the nerve to say it for certain. I'm not trying to play games. You mean too much. I didn't plan this. I'm not trying to pressure you. You just have to know that I can't feel the way I do and keep going forward when I'm not really sure how you feel."

Garrett's breath came out in a whoosh. She watched him carefully, waiting to see what he would say. His expression started to look like that of a frightened child. Her stomach knotted with dread. Impatient, she moved around her desk to the closet where she kept a small selection of clothes to wear out front when needed. Garrett stood stock still in the center of her office, completely silent. She turned to face him, her hands gripping the hanger that held a blouse.

"While you keep thinking, please let me be. I have to work." Her heart pounded in her ears.

"Delia, please…"

She shook her head. "When you're ready to maybe let me know what I mean to you, we can talk. Until then, we're right where we were before."

As she lifted her hand to gesture to the door, she saw the tremor in it and hoped he didn't notice. Garrett took a step toward her and she shook her head sharply. She stepped quickly into the small bathroom and closed the door. She carefully set her clothes on the counter and stared at herself in the mirror. Her hair was in a messy ponytail. Her shirt had stains on it from a variety of dishes she'd cooked earlier in the day. Her cheek was streaked with something and flour dusted her hair on one side. She smiled sadly. Even looking like this, Garrett kissed her. She touched her fingers to her lips, remembering the feel of his against them. If only she could trust his kisses meant something more to him.

# CHAPTER 24

Garrett stared out the windows in Gage and Marley's apartment upstairs at the lodge. He'd been staring out too many windows lately. The view here was spectacular and he couldn't even appreciate it. He turned away just as Gage walked through the door.

Gage walked straight to him and tugged him into bear hug, stepping back with a grin.

"Hey, man. How was your flight?"

"I slept the whole way here."

Gage chuckled before his expression sobered. "What's up? You don't look so good."

Garrett sighed and rolled his head from side to side, trying to ease the tension in his neck. "You know how Delia broke it off?"

Gage walked past him as he replied. "Yeah. That's why I was glad to get your message today. Thought maybe you'd gotten your head out of your ass." Gage swung the refrigerator open and held up two beers. At Garrett's nod, he opened them and tugged a stool out at the counter, gesturing for Garrett to do the same.

Garrett sat down across from him and took a swallow of beer. "I'm trying to get my head out of my ass, but it doesn't seem to be working out too well."

"What the hell could have happened between when you landed and now?"

"I went to talk to Delia, and it didn't go too well."

Gage waved his hand for Garrett to continue. Garrett once again found himself tongue-tied. Every time he tried to explain anything related to how he felt about Delia, it was like his brain went to static. He forced himself to flounder through. "Well, Delia said she loves me. And damn if I knew what to say. I swear, Gage, my brain turned off once she said that. She didn't even give me a chance to pull my shit together. She said maybe when I could let her know what she means to me and then we can talk. What the hell do I do?"

He took a gulp of beer and tried to think straight. Which had started to seem impossible when it came to Delia.

Gage was quiet for so long, Garrett started to get uncomfortable. When he looked up, he saw concern tinged with amusement in Gage's eyes.

"What?" he asked.

"Garrett, did it ever occur to you that you might need to talk about your feelings? Especially if you're going to try this whole relationship thing."

Garrett sighed and ran his hand through his hair. He was surprised his hair hadn't fallen out at this rate.

The glimmer of amusement faded from Gage's eyes. "Look, I get it. When I met Marley, it was like getting whacked upside the head. I had absolutely no idea how to deal with it. But I've had a little practice now. If there's one thing I've figured out, if someone matters a lot to you, there's no sense in trying to hide it. It won't make your feelings go away. I suppose the question you need to answer for yourself is whether you love Delia, or more specifically if you can imagine letting her pass you by. If the idea of losing her freaks you out, then you probably love her. When it comes to Delia, I don't think she's trying to pressure you. She's one of the most honest people I know. Aside from herself, she has to think about Nick. She isn't going to let someone into their lives if she's worried it might confuse Nick."

Garrett took a slow breath and another gulp of beer, the alcohol taking the edge off the panicky feeling coiled in his chest. He shook his head, tracing the label on his beer bottle. "You got the part about getting whacked upside the head right. I guess I'd better figure this one out."

"I think you already know the answer."

"Mind sharing?"

Gage hitched his brows up. "Come on, man. You know it too."

"I love her." As soon as he said it, a sense of relief followed by fear crashed through him.

"Looks like it to me."

"But how do I know for sure?"

Gage shook his head with a wry smile "Ah, the lawyer in you wants it to be black and white. You want a definite answer and want to assess all the probabilities first. It doesn't work that way."

"I don't..." Garrett started to protest, but Gage waved him off.

"Stop talking and do something. Wanna know how it looks from outside?"

"Sure."

"You're a rich, corporate lawyer who could have his pick of women. You decided to take a vacation and make some changes in your career. You have enough money that you can do that without too much trouble. Delia's beautiful and smart. She put her dreams away to move back home and raise her son because she couldn't afford to do it on her own. Of the two of you, she should be the one who's afraid to stick her neck out, but instead it's you. You're so used to calling the shots you don't know how to handle this. I'm not saying this to give you a hard time. You're my brother, so I know you're a lot more than what shows on the surface. It doesn't change the fact that if you want Delia, you're gonna have to reach out and grab her."

Garrett stared at Gage and took another gulp of beer, emptying his bottle. "When you say it that way…"

Gage stood and clapped him on the shoulder. "I gotta get downstairs and help Don repair a plumbing leak." His eyes coasted over Garrett. "Maybe you should take a shower."

*  *  *

DELIA WALKED BACK to her office much later that night. She was the last person standing tonight. It had been relentlessly busy throughout dinner. When it finally quieted, she sent the front staff home and cleaned up on her own. She relished the mundane task of clearing tables as the busy work kept her occupied. The kitchen staff had trailed out slowly. It was almost midnight when she made her way through the kitchen. Her heels clicked on the tile floor.

She trailed her hand along the steel table running through the center of the kitchen. A prickle of awareness ran up her spine.

"Delia."

Garrett's voice sent heat spiraling through her body. Her pulse stuttered and then raced ahead. She stopped and slowly turned. He stood in the doorway to the kitchen, backlit by the lights from the reception area. The kitchen was dim with only the back corner light on. Garrett had changed out of his rumpled suit. He wore a faded pair of jeans and a cotton jersey that hugged his muscled chest. She knew how his body felt under her hands. He walked slowly toward her, his eyes never leaving hers. With each step closer, her heart pounded harder and her breath came in soft pants. Emotions and desire swirled inside.

He didn't stop until he stood right in front of her. He was quiet for so long, she could hardly breathe.

"I'm sorry I've been such an idiot…"

She started to shake her head.

"It's okay. I've been trying to figure out how to explain myself. Here's the thing, I've never had a relationship. If it seems like I'm fumbling around, I am. I didn't plan on you. You have to know I never wondered if I wanted to be with you, but I didn't know what it meant. When you told me you loved me, my brain went blank." He paused and took a gulp of air. "I love you too. My assistant in Seattle told me I needed to practice saying it. I guess I didn't think it was necessary, but obviously it is."

Delia's heart soared skyward, hope unfurling its wings and swooping through her body. She hadn't realized she'd been holding her breath until she let it go. Tears welled.

Garrett took another step closer. "Are you okay?"

She nodded jerkily and swiped at her tears with the back of her hand. Now she was the one who couldn't find words.

"So tears are good?"

He settled his hands on her shoulders and slid them down her arms, the heat of his touch soothing her.

"Uh huh."

Garrett's mouth hooked on one side, his smile slowly spreading across his face. "That wasn't so bad," he said with a touch of bemusement.

"What?"

"Telling you I loved you. I feel silly now, but it scared the shit out of me."

She looked up into his eyes and bit her lip. "Me too."

# CHAPTER 25

*G*arrett's heart was hammering in his chest, adrenaline pumping through him. He was supposed to be the master of words, arguing case upon case not matter how contentious without ever breaking a sweat. Yet, faced with Delia and actually saying his feelings aloud, he turned into a bundle of nerves and adrenaline.

She looked up at him and bit her lip. "Me too."

A sense of relief washed through him on the heels of the rush of adrenaline. He looked down at her in the dim light. Her teeth dented her plump bottom lip. Her cheeks were flushed and her eyes were bright. He took a step closer, the air around them heating. In the quiet, he could hear his pulse pounding through his veins and the soft ebb and flow of her breath.

Delia's hand fell softly against his chest. He curled his around it and gave it a squeeze before sliding his palm up the side of her neck. Her pulse beat against his thumb. Time was slow and fast at once. In what felt like slow motion, he fit his mouth over hers. Suddenly, he felt as if he were caught in a flame, twisting up through and around them. Her mouth fell open on a gasp and he dove into their kiss, sweeping his tongue inside.

She flexed into him, and he let the reins loose, tugging her tight against him. He stroked his hands down her back to cup her bottom, lush and soft in his grip. Garrett couldn't get close enough fast enough and tore at her blouse. A button caught and fell when he yanked, pinging off the stainless steel table running through the kitchen. She wore a silky white bra underneath the white blouse, her nipples peaked and pushing against the fitted silk. He cupped her breasts in his hands and closed his lips over a nipple, savoring her broken gasp as he dampened the silk. He flicked the clasp of her bra and shoved it off her shoulders.

Delia pushed him back and shoved his shirt up. In seconds, the rest of their clothes were scattered on the kitchen floor. Garrett stopped and stared at her, her skin golden in the soft light emanating from the corner. She lifted her palm and stroked it down the center of his chest. She moved swiftly and leaned forward, taking his cock in her mouth. His breath came out in a strangled gasp as she knelt in front of him and commenced to drive him to the edge of his endurance with her mouth. Long, slow strokes with her tongue and deep suction when she drew him fully into her mouth. Pressure gathered inside. Just when he thought he might break, she drew away and slowly stood, a soft smile playing at her mouth.

He moved swiftly, lifting her against him and setting her on the table, stepping between her knees.

* * *

THE STAINLESS STEEL table was cool against her skin, the contrast to the heat inside of her notching it even higher. Delia looked up into Garrett's navy gaze, hot, dark and locked on her. "Your turn," he said, his gruff words sending shivers through her.

He nudged her knees apart and stroked a finger through her folds, slick with desire. Her breath broke on a moan as he slowly slipped his fingers inside her channel. He gripped her hips with his hand and tugged her closer to the edge of the table before leaning forward and bringing his mouth to join his fingers. She tumbled into sensation—his fingers sliding in and out, his tongue tracing her folds and teasing her clit. Pleasure streaked through her with each stroke of his fingers. She spun tighter and tighter inside until he exerted the slightest suction on her clit and sensation whipped through her.

With the shudders of her climax echoing, he stepped between her knees again. She felt the heated velvet of his cock nudge between her folds. He held still for a beat, long enough that the need to feel him inside of her clawed at her. At her low moan, he surged into her, seating himself deeply at once.

Holding still again, he laced his hand in her hair, angling her face up to his.

*"Delia...look at me."*

She dragged her eyes open. Only then did he begin to move. Sensation and emotion gusted through her. Her body arched into him with every stroke, craving the fullness of him inside of her—while the intimacy between them stitched tighter and tighter with every stroke, his eyes holding hers through it all. Her climax rose from the lingering spasms of the other, her legs curling tightly around his hips as she cried out.

His cry followed hers, his body arching taut like a bow before her name tore out of his throat. She slowly drifted down. Her legs loosened around his hips. His head tipped forward, his lips catching hers in a soft kiss.

They remained still for several long moments until

Garrett ran his palms down her arms. "You're getting cold," he said, his voice barely above a whisper. "Come on. Let's go to my room."

She looked up. "You have your own room again?"

His mouth hooked in a half smile. "Gage is a good brother."

# CHAPTER 26

*A* few weeks later, Delia sat at a booth in the corner of the lodge restaurant. The afternoon rush was over, and she was joining Ginger and Marley for drinks and dinner.

Ginger held her wineglass aloft. "This one's for Garrett," she said with a grin.

Marley approached their booth and slid in beside Ginger. "We're toasting Garrett?"

Ginger nodded enthusiastically. "Yup. He gets major points for getting his head out of his ass."

Delia giggled while Marley grabbed a glass and filled it. "I'm all for Garrett figuring out how awesome Delia is," Marley said with a clink of her glass with Ginger's.

Delia blushed. She still hadn't gotten used to the fact that once Garrett got over himself, he'd become prone to frequent and public displays of affection. The last few weeks since he'd flown back to Alaska had been a blur. He took her breath away and drove her to edges of passion she'd never imagined. She also enjoyed an easy comfort with him and loved watching him settle into being here. He spent most days working with Gage and her father, often bringing Nick along with them. He was somehow managing to do some long distance legal work for his practice in Seattle and making plans to start a small one here in Alaska. He planned to offer services from Diamond Creek up to Anchorage. She'd been startled when his assistant reported he was already getting requests for representation in Anchorage. Gage had explained to her Garrett's corporate work had given him a national reputation, which meant easy work here if he wanted it. He insisted he only planned to handle a few corporate cases.

Marley brushed her hair out of her face. "So, Garrett must be with Gage up on the mountain, huh?"

Delia nodded. "He said they were taking Nick for a ski this afternoon."

"Have you thought about what's next?" Ginger asked.

"What do you mean?"

"Garrett got over himself, and so did you. You're floating along in the honeymoon phase, but what's next? Is he officially moving here? Are you two moving in together? Have you talked to Nick?" Ginger waved her hand as she rattled off her questions.

Marley burst out laughing. "Oh my God. Maybe you could give her a chance to breathe and enjoy herself for a little while."

Ginger shook her head firmly. "Oh no. I need to see everything get settled. You know me and my trust issues. I apply them to all my friends."

Delia rolled her eyes. "I'm with you on wanting everything settled. All I can tell you is Garrett is officially moving here. He plans to go back to Seattle next week for a few weeks. I'll probably go down on the weekends until he can get back up here. The rest...I don't know. I'm going to talk to Nick soon because he's been asking questions about how come I'm spending the night out so much. All this time I thought it was smart not to date because it might confuse Nick, but now he's loaded with questions because I've never dated anyone since I had him."

As she spoke, the sound of feet running across the room drew her attention. She glanced up to see Nick racing across the room to their booth. His cheeks were ruddy from the cold and his dark hair windblown. Garrett and Gage entered the room behind him, moving at a more leisurely pace.

"Mom! I made it all the way down without falling!" Nick skidded across the carpeted floor, bumping against the edge of the table as he came to a stop.

"That's great!" Delia tugged him to her side for a quick hug.

Garrett reached them and ruffled Nick hair. "He did great. Even I fell once on the way down," he said with a wry grin.

Gage approached and cuffed Garrett on the shoulder. "You almost had it until you looked back at me." Gage dropped a kiss on Marley's cheek and slid into the booth beside her.

Garrett followed suit while Nick bounced between the kitchen and their booth while he wheeled extras out of the cooks. A while later, Delia waved goodbye to Ginger and watched Marley and Gage make their way to the stairs up to their apartment. She glanced to Garrett. He was in the middle of patiently listening to Nick show him his mastery of a word game on his phone. Nick looked up and caught her eyes. He paused, his eyes bouncing between her and Garrett. He suddenly looked serious. His gaze pinned to Garrett, he asked, "Do you love my mom?"

Garrett's didn't hesitate. "I do."

Delia's heart sped, a thrill of joy racing through her. Her joy was tempered with a thread of anxiety. She didn't really know how Nick would feel about Garrett becoming a more permanent part of their lives, and it worried her. She wanted him to be able to accept it and hopefully feel good about it. No matter how good it was, it was a sea change for their lives.

Nick traced the edge of the smartphone sitting on the table. He was quiet for a long moment. "Are you going away again?"

Garrett started to shake his head and stopped. "I have to go to Seattle for a little while, but I'm coming back. I'll always come back."

Delia couldn't help herself. "Nick, you don't need to worry about that."

Nick whipped his head up. "Yes, I do. My dad never came back. That makes you sad, and I don't want you to be sad again."

Her heart clenched. "Nick, honey, I'm sad about your dad because I wish he was here for you, but I'm okay."

Nick chewed the inside of his mouth as he looked between her and Garrett. Garrett eased his hand to Nick's back and stroked it slowly. "Okay."

Delia felt tears well, but she swallowed them and forced herself to breathe. Part of being a parent was holding it together at times when you felt like you might fall apart. The maelstrom of emotions wasn't always rational for adults, much less for children.

Before she could speak, Garrett did. "I understand why you might be worried. All I can say is that I plan to be with your mom for a long, long time. Maybe it's not so easy to believe that, but I'll try to show you. Okay?"

Nick looked up, his eyes wide. "Okay. Are you gonna stay with us?"

Garrett's brows hitched, an unbelieving smile curling his mouth. "Uh, well, we haven't figured everything out yet."

Nick didn't budge, his eyes holding steady. Delia started to speak, but once again Garrett beat her to it. "How about we agree that we'll talk again tomorrow?"

Nick looked to her and back to Garrett before he nodded. "Okay."

# EPILOGUE

*I*t was approaching midnight and the sun had yet to fully set though it hovered low above the mountains. A curl blew across Delia's face, the late breeze making merry with her hair and the silk of her wedding dress. Her hands were clasped tightly in Garrett's as they stood on the deck behind Last Frontier Lodge. Summer solstice, the longest day of the year, was about to mark their wedding date. She blew a puff of air to get the errant curl out of her eyes. Garrett's eyes, so somber, lightened with a half-smile. He freed one of her hands and brushed the curl out of the way, tucking it behind her ear. A hot shiver chased in the wake of his touch.

Every moment of the ceremony, she felt as if she was humming inside and out—joy, desire and intimacy dancing through her. At the feet of the mountains that had surrounded her for her entire life, Delia and Garrett were married on that almost endless summer day under the collective gaze of family and friends. The sun's bow was slow and spectacular. By the time it fell behind the mountains, the sky was a watercolor of orange and red shot through with gold.

Hours after the ceremony, Delia glanced around the lodge restaurant—a place that had once represented her lost dreams, dreams that drifted away under the mundane reality of being a single parent. Now, the restaurant linked her present with her past. Garrett was deep into a card game with his brothers, Gage and Sawyer. Sawyer had flown up from no-one-knew-where after his latest classified mission as a Navy SEAL. As if he sensed her eyes on him, Garrett looked up—electricity snapped and crackled in the air across the room. She blew him a kiss, her gaze moving on. Becca was leaning against the bar talking with their mother, Jill. Aidan McNamara, a close family friend, stood nearby and could barely keep his eyes off Becca. Delia couldn't help but wonder about those two. To say Becca was cynical about men would be an understatement. Yet, Becca snuck glances at Aidan whenever she thought no one was looking.

Nick and several other sleepy children were napping in a few booths in the corner. She walked over and brushed Nick's hair away before dropping a kiss on his forehead. When she stood, she felt a hand stroke down her back and curl around her hip. Turning her head, her eyes collided with Garrett's.

"Hey babe."

"Hey." She bit her lip when he dropped a kiss on the back of her neck.

Ginger paused by them on her way toward the bar. "When are you two making your escape?"

Delia glanced at the clock above the bar. "Soon. Have you seen my dad?"

Ginger waved to the other side of the room. "He's over there with Helen. It might be weird, but I think they'd make a great couple," she said with a grin.

Garrett followed her gaze and arched a brow. "You know, you just might have a point."

Delia considered the one lingering worry she had since she and Garrett had begun planning their life together—leaving her father to live alone in that rambling house. If he and Helen found their way to each other, it would bring him companionship and comfort, and Nick would be over-joyed. As they'd slowly gotten to know Helen, it was obvious Helen not only adored the chance to get to know her grandson, but Nick loved the extra attention.

She gave Ginger a quick hug. "We're on our way out. See you when we get back." She tugged Garrett's hand into hers and made her way across the room to her father and Helen.

"Hey, you two. We're about to head out. Nick's asleep in one of the booths over there," she said, gesturing in Nick's direction. "You have everything you need, right?"

Delia was departing for a two-week honeymoon with Garrett to the Cayman Islands. This would be the longest stretch of time she'd ever been away from Nick. It was strange she'd never thought about how it might feel to be away from him. He was going on seven years old now and would probably miss her, but he would be busy as ever with activities with her father, Marley and Gage, and any number of friends.

Don caught her eyes with a wry smile. "Hon, I've been helping you raise Nick since the day he was born. Pretty sure we can handle the next two weeks while you're gone."

"I know, Dad. I've never been gone this long, so cut me some slack."

Helen smiled softly. "He'll be just fine, dear."

Garrett squeezed her hand. "Our flight's leaving soon."

She glanced up into his navy gaze. With a quick nod, she let him lead her out of the room and into the rest of their life.

\* \* \*

GARRETT ROLLED OVER IN BED, sliding his hand over the curve of Delia's hip. "Mm," he mumbled into her neck. She was soft and warm. In the last six months, he'd come to absolutely adore waking up beside her every day. After a quintessentially romantic honeymoon in the tropics, they'd returned to Diamond Creek. He'd settled into a life he'd have once never imagined. They'd purchased a home on a bluff overlooking Kachemak Bay. He'd gone from a glamorous, relentlessly busy life in Seattle to a much quieter and messier life on the breathtaking coast of Alaska. He'd traded the big city for a small, quirky community.

The pulse of this tight-knit community called to a part of him he'd never known he had. As he'd originally envisioned, he still kept his practice in Seattle, but rarely flew back. He handled most of his work online and only went there when absolutely necessary. His legal work in Alaska was much more varied than he ever could have guessed. He handled corporate cases in Anchorage, small criminal cases in Diamond Creek and other nearby communities, and civil cases ranging from environmental issues to fishing disputes. He was never bored.

A while later, Delia hurried around the kitchen, coffee cup in hand as she slapped a sandwich together for Nick's lunch.

"Mom! I can't find my homework!" Nick called out from down the hall.

"Got it," Garrett said. He'd quickly discovered that while Nick was reliable about completing his homework, he routinely lost track of it once it was done. Garrett had become the expert at helping him find it.

After walking Nick through his evening before, he found it by the sink in the hall bathroom. When he returned to the kitchen, the small folder held aloft, Nick ran over and threw his arms around Garrett's waist. Garrett's heart clenched. Just last week, the court had finalized his adoption of Nick. Garrett had never expected that, but Nick's biological father had died in a car accident a few months after their wedding. He'd already considered himself Nick's father in every way that mattered, and he hated seeing Nick's sadness at learning the father he never knew had died. The adoption had offered an odd sense of completion Garrett hadn't known he was seeking.

Moments later, he watched Nick climb on the bus. Delia was loading the dishwasher. She stood and closed it quickly. When she turned, she headed toward the hall. Garrett stepped in front of her, curling his hands around her arms. She stopped abruptly and looked up. Her soft blue eyes caught his. She took a breath. He felt the tension ease from her body. "What's the rush?" he asked, a jolt of lust streaking through him.

It still startled him how much he wanted her. If anything, the depth of his desire for her had grown deeper, along with his love for her.

"I forgot to get the pastries ready last night because we were so busy, so I have to get to work early…"

Garrett caught her lips in a kiss. "No you don't."

"Garrett, I can't be late just because…"

"I called Harry already. He said your new assistant is doing great, and you can take the morning off."

Delia bit her lip, and he was a goner. He swore she did it on purpose sometimes, and he didn't give a damn. He tugged her close and lifted her to the table. "Now, where was I?"

He caught her giggle with a kiss.

Thank you for reading Love at Last - I hope you loved
Garrett & Delia's story!

For more steamy, small town romance, Becca & Aidan's
story is next in Just This Once. Aidan McNamara is a sexy,
alpha SEAL who's been half in love with Becca Hamilton for
years. One night turns into so much more.
Tall, dark, sexy, and oh-so-alpha, don't miss Aidan's story!

Keep reading for a sneak peek!

Be sure to sign up for my newsletter for the latest news,
teasers & more! Click here to sign up:
http://jhcroixauthor.com/subscribe/

# SNEAK PEEK: JUST THIS ONCE BY J.H. CROIX; ALL RIGHTS RESERVED

## Chapter 1

THE THWACK of the windshield wipers was steady as Becca Hamilton drove along the highway. It was approaching midnight, much later than she planned to be on her way to her parents' home in Bellingham, Washington. She had yet another late night at work in Seattle, but she'd promised her mother she'd be there for the weekend. After failing to come through on the same promise last weekend, she was bound and determined to get there tonight. The visibility was crap with fog and rainy mist encompassing the road. She might as well have been in the middle of a cloud. She rolled her shoulders in a weak attempt to ease the tension bundled in them.

Glancing at the clock, she estimated she had another hour before she made it to Bellingham. Suddenly, lights flashed in front of her as she came around a corner, much too close for comfort. Before she could think and blinded by the lights, she yanked the steering wheel and swerved to avoid the vehicle coming straight at her. She felt the other car bounce off of hers and heard a loud screech before her car tumbled into the ditch. She came to a thudding stop with her car on its side.

Stunned for a second, she started to scramble and tried to climb out before it occurred to her she might want to take stock of her situation first. She froze and glanced around. Rain continued to fall, her windshield wipers carrying on as if nothing had happened. She looked up toward the road to see the taillights of the car that ran her off the road disappearing into the wet darkness.

"Great, just great," she muttered. "Run me off the road and leave. Dammit!" She adjusted her position, so her hips rested on the console between the driver and passenger seats. She mentally scanned her body and didn't sense any significant injuries. Her shoulder had jammed against the ceiling. She figured she'd be sore from the impact by morning, but all in all, she seemed okay. The pressing issue was she was alone in the dark, rainy night stuck in a ditch.

If there was one thing Becca hated, it was asking for help. It ranked right up there with dating. She hated it so much she actually pondered the likelihood that she could somehow get her car upright again on her own. Mid-thought, her rational brain kicked in. *Are you out of your damn mind? Don't confuse yourself with a superhero. There is NO way you can get your car out of this ditch by yourself.* She smiled wryly to herself. There were times she needed to swallow her pride and accept she needed help. They were few and far between, but this definitely qualified.

She flicked on the interior light and searched for her purse, which held her phone. It had fallen to the passenger side on the floor. Far out of her reach. She started maneuvering to reach it when there was a knock on her window. She scrambled back up and managed to reach the button to open the window. As the blurry glass rolled down, a familiar face loomed in the rainy darkness. Aidan McNamara, the absolute last person she wanted to see her like this. Aidan was a family friend through her older brother Gage. They'd served together in the Navy SEAL's. Aidan was a woman's dream if one liked tall, dark, sexy-as-hell military types who tended to save the day so often it was annoying. Even under these circumstances, Becca's pulse raced at the sight of him. As much as it drove her insane, her body had all kinds of ideas about Aidan.

"Becca?" Aidan's brows hitched up when he saw her.

"It's me."

"Are you okay? Let's get you out of there."

Aidan didn't bother to ask what happened, but instantly went into action. After he did a quick circle around her car to make sure it was safe to pull her out, he opened her door and reached in for her. He ignored her protests as he lifted her out. Next thing she knew, she was in his strong arms, the rain falling softly around them. He adjusted her weight in arms. Becca shivered and couldn't help the tiny curl of comfort that snuck through her. A corner of her savored feeling protected like this. Aidan had the disconcerting tendency to elicit this feeling in her. She pushed against it like a cat swatting its paw and wiggled.

"Put me down," she demanded. Her voice sounded prickly, and she didn't care.

She heard his sigh. "Becca, it's more work to put you down right here than it is to carry you. The ground's like mush here. Let's get to the road, and I'll put you down."

She bit her lip and stayed quiet. Aidan's embrace was strong and sure. She could feel his muscles flex against her body as he stepped carefully up the incline. Her pulse galloped and heat slid through her veins. Why, oh why, did this man have to affect her like this? She'd sworn off men after her fiancée had dumped her two days before their wedding. That had been three years ago. Since then, she'd had no trouble completely ignoring men. Except for Aidan. He had this unerring ability to make her flushed and flustered simply by existing.

He reached the road and carefully eased her down. His black sedan was pulled to the side of the road, its lights illuminating them. She glanced up. Of course, Aidan had come to her aid without bothering to put a jacket on. His button-down shirt was clinging to his muscled chest and arms. His black hair was damp from the rain. His blue eyes were bright in the small circle of light cast around them. His strong features were shadowed. His blade of a nose crooked the tiniest bit in one spot. She'd always wanted to ask how he broke it, but she never had. With his career as a Navy SEAL, she surmised he'd had many brushes with injury.

He gestured to her car. "Need me to get anything for you?"

"Oh, um. I can get my stuff. Let me…" She started to turn and walk back into the ditch when she felt his hand curl around her arm.

His grip was strong and implacable. "I'll get it. You seem to have gotten out of this without getting hurt, but I'm not letting you go back down there. Where's your stuff?"

"Oh my God! Don't be all tough with me. I'm fine. I can…"

"Becca," Aidan said, his tone low with warning. "Gage will let me have it if I let you climb back down there and you somehow get hurt. We don't know if your car's stable where it is, and it's a mud pit. Just tell me what I need to find."

She wanted to argue, but she bit it back. She was cold, tired and wet. The shock of getting bounced into a ditch by another car was starting to set in. On the heels of a deep breath, she managed to nod. "Okay. My purse fell on the floor in the front. My bag should be in the backseat."

Aidan nodded and turned away quickly. She waited by the side of the road. She heard him moving around, but she couldn't see much in the dark. Her car engine and lights were turned off before she heard a door slam, and he climbed back up to her side. Her purse and small overnight bag were hanging from his shoulder. She followed him to his car. Somehow he beat her to the passenger side and held the door for her. Once she was seated, he handed her purse over and put her bag in the backseat.

His car was warm. She held her hands in front of the heater and rubbed them together. Of course, he drove a luxury sedan. She had no idea what kind of car it was, but the seats were soft, supple leather, and the engine hummed so quietly she could barely hear it. When Aidan climbed inside, he looked over at her.

"What happened?" he asked.

"A car came around the corner in my lane. I swerved to avoid them, and they bumped me on the way. Next thing I know, I was in the ditch." She hugged her arms around her waist, her teeth chattering slightly from the cold.

He reached behind her and pulled something forward. "Here, put this on. You got pretty wet." He handed her a sweatshirt.

Without thinking, she pulled it over her head, sighing once it fell around her. It held a subtle woodsy scent. The sweatshirt nearly swallowed her whole, but she tugged it close, savoring the warmth. She could hardly let herself think it, but she loved that it held his scent.

"Thanks. I didn't realize how cold I was."

Aidan nodded, his eyes still on her. "Should I take you to the hospital to get checked out?"

She shook her head quickly. "No! I'm fine. I got bounced against the roof when my car rolled in the ditch, but I'm fine. I do *not* need to go to the hospital."

He was quiet for a long moment before he nodded. "Okay. Let me make a call to get your car towed."

Before she could say anything, he'd tapped a button on the screen in the center of his dashboard.

"Hey, boss. What can we do for you?" A man's voice came through the car speakers clearly.

"Hey, George. I need you guys to arrange for a towing company to come get Becca Hamilton's car out of a ditch. It's about twenty minutes north from our office. I'll wait with her until you guys get here, then you can take it from there."

"We'll head up there right now. Are you on I-5 or Route 9?"

"Route 9. Look for my car."

"Got it."

The line clicked.

"You didn't have to..." Becca started to say.

"We're not leaving your car here." Aidan glanced out the window as another car drove by, its headlights blurry in the rain. "The fastest tow company can't get here sooner. This way, George will wait with your car and make sure everything's taken care of. In the meantime, where were you headed?"

Aidan didn't entertain her weak attempt to tell him he didn't need to have his company handle getting her car towed. After Aidan retired as a Navy SEAL, he started a private security company in Seattle. The company quickly developed an excellent reputation. Becca encountered him and his employees frequently in her work as a prosecutor for the Seattle District Court. She hadn't thought through what she was going to do about her car, but it chafed at her to have Aidan step in and handle things like this.

Warmth was starting to seep through her bones between the heat in his car and his sweatshirt. She took a breath and tried to gather her thoughts. Being this close to Aidan was discombobulating. She preferred to be somewhere she could take a step back and create enough distance between them, so her heart didn't pound so hard and heat didn't slide through her veins. To regain control, she latched onto her annoyance.

"You don't have to step in and save the day, you know? I'm perfectly capable of calling a tow company and waiting for them to come. I appreciate you stopped, but..."

She paused for a breath, realizing her words were flying out of her mouth. She was flustered and disoriented. Between her unexpected roll into the ditch and Aidan's appearance, she was off kilter in more ways than one.

Aidan appeared to be waiting. She glanced sideways to find his eyes on her, inscrutable in the dim light inside the car. After another long beat, he spoke. "Becca, I'm not trying to save the day. I didn't do anything I wouldn't do for a stranger. I saw your car in the ditch and stopped to see if I could help." He gestured to the window. "It's rainy and cold out and going on midnight. I can't in good conscience just leave you here. I have no doubt you'd take care of yourself if I hadn't happened along. Maybe you don't feel the same way, but I consider you a friend. I'm not leaving a friend alone on the highway in this weather. Your brothers would never let me hear the end of it if I did."

She knew what he said was true. He would stop to help anyone because that's the kind of man he was. She just hated the fact that she needed help and the one man who somehow got under her skin happened to be the man to stop and help. She glanced out the window. The pace of the rain had picked up, shifting from a heavy mist to something close to pouring rain. It felt like they were in a warm, dry island inside his car. The space compressed. Awareness prickled along her skin. Aidan was no more than a foot away from her. Darting her eyes sideways, they landed on his hand resting on the steering wheel—a strong, muscled and masculine hand.

When she brought her eyes to his, they coasted over her face—assessing, measuring. She could barely breathe and somehow had to get through the next twenty minutes until George arrived to wait with her car.

Aidan shifted in his seat, one of his hands falling to the console between them. "Have I don't something to offend you?" he asked suddenly.

She could tell by his tone that he was genuinely curious. She shook her head. Because how could she explain that all he'd done was to be the one and only man who made her forget her promise she'd never let a man get to her again? It wouldn't be so bad if he were some random guy she encountered once in a blue moon. No, he had to go and be one of Gage's best friends and a friend to her entire family. She couldn't avoid him even if she tried.

"Well, then what is it? Every time I'm around you, you seem annoyed."

Instead of dropping the topic, he kept going. Her body was a jumble of nerves, electricity emanating from him and coiling around her, setting her nerves alight and heat notching higher and higher.

"I'm not annoyed." Maybe she could try to opposite approach. Say the opposite of everything she felt, and the feelings would go away.

He arched a brow, a smile playing at the corners of his mouth. "Really?"

Annoyance arced higher. "No, I'm not! But I'm about to be."

Aidan chuckled. She couldn't help the laugh that bubbled in response. She turned to him and collided with his gaze. In a flash, the air around them hummed with heat. His smile faded. Becca could hardly breathe. She held still, her heart battering against her ribcage. Before she knew what happened, he leaned across the console, erasing the distance between them.

She opened her mouth to say something and his lips came against hers. Soft and sure at once, he fit his mouth over hers. She froze, but for the life of her she couldn't pull away. Not when her body cried out for more, craving to get as close as she could to imprint herself against his body the way his lips were now molded to hers. He angled his head, his tongue tracing her lips. Her breath broke on a low moan, and he captured it by deepening his kiss. His tongue delved inside, hers responding by tangling with his. The kiss went from a tentative exploration to explosive. Heat surged through her in waves as she nearly crawled across the console to get closer. His hand stroked up her neck, lacing into the hair at her nape. His thumb brushed across the beat of her pulse, which went wild at the feel of his calloused skin against her.

Oh. My. God. He felt so good—*so, so, sooo* good. All this time, she hadn't allowed herself to wonder what it would feel like to kiss Aidan. Every time her body considered it, she ran away from the thought, trying to shove her body's desire into a box where she could lock it up and pretend it didn't exist. Now that she'd tasted him, she didn't think she could ever forget. He kissed the way he did everything— with complete confidence. He alternated with strong, commanding strokes of his tongue and soft, devastating kisses when he pulled back incrementally.

Somehow, her hand was stroking into the curls at the base of his skull, his hair damp against her fingers. He tore his mouth away, his lips coasting down her neck, his rough stubble scraping her skin, making her arch into him. Hot, wet kisses blazed a trail along the edge of her collarbone and dipped into the vee of her blouse. Her nipples were tight, peaked in desire. She wanted to feel more, more of everything. She wanted his touch on every inch of her body. *Now.*

* * *

AIDAN LOOSENED his hand in Becca's silky brown hair and dragged the back of his fingers along behind his lips. She tasted so damn good, like sweet cream with a twist—exactly how he'd have guessed. She tried to blend in and not stand out, but she was too damn beautiful for that. Her kisses gave her away—passionate and wild. She threw herself into their kiss, her body twining against his in the cramped space of his car. He licked into the valley between her breasts. He couldn't resist sliding his hand around to cup her breast, its weight heavy against his palm. Her nipple tightened under his touch.

Suddenly, there was a sharp knock at the window. He swore and leaned away from Becca. Her eyes slammed into his—her beautiful blue eyes. He'd stared into those eyes many times, always struggling to rein in the impulse to kiss her. Her eyes were a deep shade of blue, usually guarded with a hint of distrust, the shield she hid behind. At the moment, she looked as stunned as he felt. The shield had fallen and what he saw there slammed him in the gut. Vulnerability, confusion and desire swirled together for a split second before she shuttered them. She pulled back swiftly.

At another knock on the window, he turned and tapped the button for it to open a sliver. George's grin met him. "Hey boss. We're here."

"I noticed. Give me a sec, okay?"

At George's nod, he closed the window and turned back to Becca. She'd firmly planted herself as far away as she could, mashed up against the door with her arms crossed. She stared straight ahead. Her lips were plump and swollen and her cheeks flushed. Her pulse beat rapidly in her neck, her skin illuminated from the lights of George's car behind them.

She spoke rapidly. "I don't know what that was, but let's forget about it. I'm not thinking clearly and you're not either. How about I hitch a ride back to Seattle with your guys? They won't mind, right?"

Aidan shook his head. Maybe he hadn't planned to kiss Becca, but he'd wanted to ever since he'd first laid eyes on her almost ten years ago. Back then, she was a mere twenty-three years old and a very studious law student. He could still recall the first time he saw her. He was on a break between missions with his team. Gage had invited him and another friend, Matt, to a family barbecue. Becca had been seated at a picnic table, her glossy brown hair hiding her face as she studied a book. She was already in her second year in law school. Then, he was a young twenty-eight years old and deep in the swagger of being a Navy SEAL. He hadn't even noticed her at first, but sat down at the table to rest his knee, which was sore from a fall. Becca had finally looked from her book and pushed her glasses up on her nose. He felt like he'd been punched. She was so damn beautiful, he'd simply stared at her.

After several long moments of silence, Becca's mouth had curled into a smile. "You must be Aidan," she'd said. All he'd been able to do was nod. Somehow, he'd regained the ability to speak and carried on a semi-normal conversation with her, all the while reminding himself he couldn't try to make a play for Gage's little sister. Not to mention that he wasn't interested in making a play in a casual way. He'd looked at her—at the gorgeous fall of brown hair, her sharp blue eyes behind her cat-shaped glasses, and her full pink mouth—and he'd wanted to lift her in his arms and carry her away to be with him forever. But he couldn't do that because he was home between missions. He was already scheduled to leave with his team in a few short days on another classified mission. In the intervening years, she'd gotten engaged and dumped by her fiancée. He'd learned that bitter news from Gage on the mission when their friend Matt had died.

Ten long years later, Aidan finally kissed Becca. Instead of it being planned and carried out meticulously, he'd impulsively kissed her in his car on the side of the road. His heart pounding, he gathered himself and looked at her.

"I won't forget it, and neither will you. Stop pretending." Her eyes swung to his, wide and startled. "I didn't plan it this way, but I've wanted to kiss you for too damn long. Don't pretend you didn't want it too. I'm going to get out and make sure those guys don't need anything from me. Then, I'm taking you wherever you need to go. We can talk on the way. Or not. But for God's sake, don't act like this was nothing. Because it damn well wasn't and you know it."

Becca stared at him and chewed her lip. He thought his heart might pound its way out of his chest, but he forced himself to breathe. He was afraid he'd played his cards too fast, but he'd kept his feelings under wraps for so long, his restraint was weak. When she finally nodded slowly, he let his breath go.

He climbed out into the rain, which soaked him instantly. After checking in with George and Dale and conferring with the towing company on the way, he climbed back in his sedan. Becca turned to him.

"You're soaked! I don't imagine you have a towel in here, huh?"

"Actually, I do." He reached into the back and curled his hand around the handle of a black case, which held first aid and other supplies. A small, highly absorbent towel was tucked in the corner. He whipped it out and dried his face and hair.

Becca started laughing. "Only you would have a case like that. Or maybe Gage," she said as she rolled her eyes.

"Gage definitely has one. Carryover from our military days." He tossed the towel into the back seat and eyed her. "Okay, I don't think we ever got to the part about where you were headed."

"You can just take me back to Seattle." Her shoulders hunched on a sigh.

"I'll take you wherever you need to go. I know you weren't driving home at midnight."

"I was on my way to Bellingham to see my parents. I was supposed to go last weekend, but it got too late, so I promised I'd be there this weekend. But now it's past midnight, it's pouring and if you take me, I don't know how I'll get back home."

Aidan shrugged. "We're headed the same place. Did you forget my sister lives in Bellingham?"

She glanced at the clock. "Okay. You sure you don't mind?"

"Not at all." He didn't wait for her to reconsider and put his car in gear and slowly pulled off the side of the highway.

Once they were on the way north, he glanced to the side. Becca was no longer plastered against the door. Her shoulders had relaxed and she leaned back in the passenger seat, curling her feet up under her knees. He elected to keep conversation casual. He sensed if he referenced their kiss or anything he'd said afterwards, she might shut down. The rainy drive passed swiftly. The lights of Bellingham glimmered through the rain. Aidan had been to her parents' home a number of times, so he made his way there on memory. When he pulled up in the circular drive, he cut his lights and climbed out quickly. Becca wore a rueful smile when he opened the passenger side door.

"You just love opening doors, don't you?"

He shrugged. "My mother was old-fashioned. She insisted on manners."

She nodded and climbed out, stretching as she stood. He snagged her bag from the back and walked by her side to the front door. The rain fell around them. Her eyes were tired. He sensed the only reason she wasn't her usual prickly self with him was she was too tired for it and her defenses were down. A surge of protectiveness washed through him. He hated that ever since her asshole of a fiancée had dumped her two days before the wedding, she'd become bitter and prickly like a cactus if anyone got too close.

She looked up at him, her lashes spiky from the rain. "So…?"

"Can I stop by tomorrow?"

She nodded. He didn't wait and dipped his head to catch her lips. He wanted more, so much more, than the quick kiss he allowed himself. But somehow he'd managed to bumble his way through his impulsive kiss with her earlier, and he didn't want to push too far, too fast with her. She was well-defended and with good reason. Her lips were so soft and supple, he almost lost his hold on the thin thread of control he had. He forced himself to step back. "I'll call you."

AVAILABLE NOW!

Just This Once

GO HERE to sign up for information on new releases: http://jhcroixauthor.com/subscribe/

# FIND MY BOOKS

*T*hank you for reading Love at Last! I hope you enjoyed the story. If so, you can help other readers find my books in a variety of ways.

1) Write a review!

2) Sign up for my newsletter, so you can receive information about upcoming new releases & receive a FREE copy of one of my books: http://jhcroixauthor.com/subscribe/

3) Like and follow my Amazon Author page at https://amazon.com/author/jhcroix

4) Follow me on Bookbub at https://www.bookbub.com/authors/j-h-croix

5) Follow me on Twitter at https://twitter.com/JHCroix

6) Like my Facebook page at https://www.facebook.com/jhcroix

\* \* \*

**LAST FRONTIER LODGE Novels**
Christmas on the Last Frontier

Love at Last
Just This Once
Falling Fast
Stay With Me
When We Fall
Hold Me Close
Crazy For You
**Into The Fire Series**
Burn For Me
Slow Burn
Burn So Bad
Hot Mess
Burn So Good
**Brit Boys Sports Romance**
The Play
Big Win
Out Of Bounds
Play Me
**Diamond Creek Alaska Novels**
When Love Comes
Follow Love
Love Unbroken
Love Untamed
Tumble Into Love
Christmas Nights
**Catamount Lion Shifters**
Protected Mate
Chosen Mate
Fated Mate
Destined Mate
A Catamount Christmas
**Ghost Cat Shifters**
The Lion Within
Lion Lost & Found

# ACKNOWLEDGMENTS

Yet again, a shout out to my husband who cheers me on, listens to plot ideas and graciously gives me the space and time to write. Many thanks to my editor, Laura Kingsley, for holding me to a high standard. Clarise Tan at CT Cover Creations is responsible for my stunning covers. And my readers: thank you from the bottom of my heart for your support!

# ABOUT THE AUTHOR

Bestselling author J. H. Croix lives in a small town in the historical farmlands of Maine with her husband and two spoiled dogs. Croix writes steamy contemporary romance with strong independent women and rugged alpha men who aren't afraid to show some emotion. Her love for quirky small-towns and the characters that inhabit them shines through in her writing. Take a walk on the wild side of romance with her bestselling novels!

*Places you can find me:*
jhcroixauthor.com
jhcroix@jhcroix.com

Made in the USA
Columbia, SC
26 October 2020